ALSO BY MICHAEL LEALI

The Civil War of Amos Abernathy

MATTEO

MICHAEL LEALI

HARPER
An Imprint of HarperCollins*Publishers*

For my wonderful siblings and their partners

ONE

Every year on my birthday, I ask for the same story. After we celebrate with a homemade Italian dinner, a massive slice of cannoli cake, and a leaning tower of presents, I crawl into bed and Mom and Dad tell me about the night I showed up in their lives. Maybe it's a little corny, but it's my favorite birthday tradition.

"Let's see." Dad pulls his leg onto my bed. "You're what? Twenty-three now?"

"*Eleven*." I smirk. "You're so weird."

"Really?" He tousles my dark curls. "I'm pretty sure there's some stubble on that chin."

I shove his hand away. Mom laughs. "Go on, Vinny. Tell the story."

"Right, so, *eleven* years ago, Mom and I couldn't have kids. We tried *everything*." Dad takes Mom's hand in his. "We'd almost given up hope."

"But you didn't," I say. The only thing I hate about my story, the story of Matteo Lorenzini, is that it starts sad. Part of me always wants to rush to the end, but it's never as satisfying when we do.

Dad grins. "No, but we were out of options. At least, to have a baby in a traditional sense. So there I was, eleven years ago, on break at the fire station and I had babies on the brain. It was a little after midnight. I needed to shake off the dust of the day, sort out my thoughts. I wasn't thinking about where I was going, but my feet took me to the old oak in the park."

I pull the blanket up to my chin. "Just like magic."

Mom winks at me. "*Just* like it."

"It was a clear night, all stars overhead," Dad goes on. "I looked up at the tree, and all the stories my dad told me when I was a boy came rushing back. How the tree hears prayers. How it watches over us. I'd believed him as kid, but as I got older—well, sometimes life makes it hard to believe in stuff like that."

My breath sticks in my throat. Aside from my birthday, Dad never talks about Grandpa. He and my grandma—she passed when I was little—got divorced when Dad was about my age. Then Grandpa left town, and Dad hasn't heard from him since.

Now Grandpa's come up *twice* in one night and I can tell it's weighing heavily on Dad. You see, the Lorenzinis have another tradition: on the oldest son's (or *only* son's) eleventh birthday, the legendary family baseball bat gets passed down. Grandpa gave it to Dad, and now he's given it to me. It's a golden honey color, worn smooth in spots. When I first held it, I could have sworn it was warm, like all the Lorenzini men before me had only just let go. I was so excited. Baseball's a big deal for Lorenzini men. Like HUGE. And now *I'm* a part of that legacy.

Mom rests her hand on Dad's shoulder and squeezes gently. His muscles relax. I don't think he realized he'd tensed up. "What did you do next?" I ask, hoping to keep his mind off sad memories.

He blinks a couple times before snapping back to the story. "Sounds silly, but I started crying. Then I leaned my head to the tree and talked. The trunk scratched my lips, that's how close I was to it. My tears fell into the grooves where the bark split. I said, 'I don't know if you can hear me, but all my wife and I want—'"

"'Is a child,'" I finish for him. Can't help myself.

Dad bops my nose, which I'm getting *way* too old for. "Exactly."

Mom scoots closer to him. "What your dad *didn't* know was that earlier that day, I'd done the very same thing."

Yesss. These are the twists and turns I am so here for. "What made *you* go to the tree?" I ask.

"A little voice." She points to her heart. "Right in here."

"Did you cry too?"

"Enough to water the darn tree for a whole year."

"Then what?" I say, even though I already know.

"Well," Dad goes on, "I brushed myself off and wiped my face dry. Didn't want the guys seeing me upset. Then I walked back to the station kind of quiet but more hopeful than I'd felt in a while. On the way back, I texted your mom that I loved her."

Mom twists the wedding band on her finger. "I still remember getting that text. I'd been tossing and turning. My mind just wouldn't settle."

"It's like you knew, right?" I say.

"I think so." She tucks a strand of curly, dark brown, almost black hair behind her ear. "All that night, the strangest energy filled my bones. I just kept pacing. Like I knew I had to get ready for something." She turns to Dad. "Go on. Tell the rest."

He clears his throat. "So there I was, walking back from the park. I stopped dead in my tracks when I saw it. On the firehouse steps, there was this wooden basket filled with rags thin as leaves. And snuggled up underneath them was a baby."

I sit up and lean forward. Finally, the star of the story makes his grand entrance! "What did the baby—I mean, what did *I* look like?"

"Absolutely perfect. The smallest, roundest nose, bright red in the chilly air. A little curl of black hair. Itty bitty lips pressed together like you were 'bout to sneeze." Dad sighs. "I picked you up and held you close. I can still smell that new baby smell." He breathes deeply. "I knew who you were straightaway—our son, the one we'd wanted for so long."

"And no one else ever claimed me?" I ask. I know no one did, but I like to hear them say it.

"No birth parents ever came forward," says Mom. "But we knew. You were ours. Our perfect little boy. You were always meant for us."

My shoulders sink back into my pillow as I yawn. "Just like magic."

"Just like magic," they both say.

They kiss my forehead and whisper, "I love you," before they turn out the light and close the door on the first night of my eleventh year.

The year that everything is about to change.

CREEKSIDE DOCUMENTARY TRANSCRIPT #1

SUBJECT: MAYOR MEYERS

. . . .

MATTEO LORENZINI

Thanks for meeting with us today, Mayor Meyers.

MAYOR MEYERS

My pleasure. What can I do for you kids?

AZURA GONZALEZ

Matteo and I, we're putting together a documentary about Creekside for the bicentennial celebration at the end of April. We were wondering if you could tell us a little about the town?

MAYOR MEYERS

My favorite subject.

MATTEO LORENZINI

Mine too. I love Creekside stories.

AZURA GONZALEZ

And I love filming them. That's why we make such a good team.

MAYOR MEYERS

I can see that. (Laughs) What an honor to have such enthu-siastic, young documentarians working to celebrate our heritage! I look forward to seeing the final product.

MATTEO LORENZINI

Us too! So! (Shuffles papers) What can you tell us about Creekside?

MAYOR MEYERS

Well, Creekside is an old town with a long history. We take pride in who we are and where we've come from. We're more than an hour's drive from the nearest city. Cornfields and prairie grass on all sides. Houses with little white fences frame the downtown. There's a fire station and a post office, a cinema and a library. (Points out window) But what we're best known for is the old oak out in Creekside Park.

AZURA GONZALEZ

Why's the tree so special?

MAYOR MEYERS

That oak's been around as long as this town. Our history is wound up in its roots. More memories circling that trunk than anywhere else. Some say it's the beating heart of Creekside.

MATTEO LORENZINI

Is that what you think?

MAYOR MEYERS

I say it's more than that. I'd say it's our very soul. (Sighs)
That's why it guts me that it's dying.

TWO

This is *my* year. The year I prove to Dad and Omar and Coach Mathis that I'm good enough. You see, I've been watching major league baseball with Dad as long as I can remember. We're Cubs fans all the way, but Dad might be even more obsessed with the Blue Whales. They were his little league team growing up. He always says his years with them were "the sugar in the otherwise bitter coffee" that was his childhood.

Playing for the Blue Whales has always been my goal. Thing is, I didn't make the team last year—which epically sucked. Not only did I let Dad down, but one of my used-to-be best friends, Omar Jones, *did* make the team and things haven't been the same between us since.

If there's one thing I don't do, though, it's give up. So this whole past year, I've practiced throwing and batting and running sprints with Dad. I busted it right up to try-outs, and I'm glad I did. They were just as hard the second time around, but this year I kept pace in the sprints and caught every pop fly in the outfield. Now I'm a Blue Whale, just like Dad was.

Still, I've got a sneaking suspicion I barely made the team. Even with all the practice, I'm not the best batter. Every guy on the team can outhit me. Part of me wonders if Coach Mathis only let me on because I'm Dad's kid. But I haven't let up training with Dad, and I've gotten better since tryouts, so I'm hoping I can really bring it to our first game today.

I've been lying in bed awhile now, playing through the innings in my head: how I'll stand when I bat, how I'll position my glove. I've got to do everything right.

On my nightstand, next to the fishbowl where my goldfish, Cricket, loops around, my alarm clock flashes a quarter past eight. "Oh shoot!" It's later than I thought. I leap out of bed. Only forty-five minutes before the game starts! Time to get my game face on.

I stretch my arms to the ceiling and say in Cricket's direction, "I totally got this, right?"

Cricket blows a bubble and swishes away.

"Thanks for the vote of confidence."

I run my fingers through my curls. Then I check myself over in the mirror as I button up my blue baseball jersey. My twiggy, white arms dangle at my sides. I flex, hoping muscles will puff up, but all I get are wormier veins. Cringey.

Some of the other guys on my team, kids I've known all my life, they've started to change. They're getting taller. Bigger. They have actual *biceps*. What I wouldn't give for a few more inches, for my shoulders to fill my shirt. Maybe then I could throw farther, hit harder.

I may not be a Lorenzini by blood, but I *am* a Lorenzini, and I'm not going to let our legacy down. Even if I'm not as good as the other guys yet, I'll get there. It's my destiny, right? Before I head downstairs, I rub the family bat for luck. C'mon, dead Lorenzinis! Help a guy out!

"Don't you look adorable," Mom says as I walk into the kitchen. "You ready for the game?"

"Ready as I'll ever be," I say, digging my spoon into a bowl of buttery farina.

Dad walks in, newspaper in hand. "There's my little man. Looking sharp." He sets the newspaper down and grabs the aluminum baseball bat resting on top of my gear bag. He wraps his fingers around the handle, two fists stacked one on top of the other. "Remember the grip I taught you, okay? Watch how Tyler Sudbury does it. Kid's a natural."

I swallow and gulp down some milk. "Yeah, I know, Dad."

I can't stand when he tells me to watch what the other kids do. Tyler especially. What he really means is that he wants me to be like Tyler Sudbury. To *be* Tyler Sudbury. Which is annoying because Tyler's a giant jerk. Every time

Dad says something like that, it hurts a little more. I'm just me, and I'm trying my best.

But it's been like this with everything I've ever done. During karate, Dad was like, "See how Tommy punches?" And then at soccer practice, he kept saying, "Jeffrey's got it; look at how he kicks the ball with the side of his foot." Even in pottery class it was "What if you tried making a pot like Stevie's?"

Dad's trying to help, but it just feels like, no matter what I do, I can't do anything right. Like I'm never enough. Some other boy is always doing it better.

But today I'll show them all what I'm made of.

CREEKSIDE DOCUMENTARY TRANSCRIPT #2

SUBJECT: COACH MATHIS

. . . .

MATTEO LORENZINI
Tell us how you started coaching baseball.

COACH MATHIS
*Started? Sheesh. I've been at this so long I almost forget I had
to "start" at all. (Laughs) Well, to me, baseball's always been
about belonging to something bigger than yourself. I wanted
to give back to my community and create a space for kids to
grow together, weather the wins and losses—*

MATTEO LORENZINI
But mostly wins, right?

COACH MATHIS
(Winks) Bingo.

THREE

By the second inning my pumped-up, feel-good vibes are already running low. I'm on the bench between Tyler and Omar, and it's all kinds of awkward. Well, *I'm* awkward. And I can't get my knee to stop bouncing. It's like I've forgotten how to talk to Omar, and Tyler, well, who in their right mind *wants* to talk to him? All morning he's gone on and on about this super-exclusive baseball camp he's going to this summer. Like I said: annoying.

The thing about Omar is that he's just as good at baseball as Tyler, but he doesn't brag about it. He's confident, not arrogant, which is one of the things I like—*liked*—most about him.

Now that I'm a Blue Whale too, I can't figure out if we're friends again. Omar's been acting friendly, but it's not like it was. He's changed. He's quieter, and he looks more grown up. Which is weird. But in a good way. Which makes me *feel* weird. But in a good way.

Ever since our first practice, when he actually acknowledged my existence again, even though he's had tons of chances at school, I get all sweaty and blushy around him, which I think has got something to do with the fact that I can't stop staring at his face. Not just because it's different, but because it's . . . cute?

Okay. Now I'm *definitely* blushing and not at all focused on the game, which is the important thing. *Come on, Matteo. Stop looking at Omar. Today's about baseball. BASEBALL.*

Behind the dugout, the crowd—mostly our parents—cheers as Tyler gets up to bat. His rosy-white wrists whip the bat around as he warms up. Then he grinds his cleats into the dusty ground and hocks a wad of spit into the grass. So gross.

The crowd whoops for him. "That's my boy!" Miles Sudbury, Tyler's dad, shouts.

Tyler smirks at the stands before facing the pitcher. We're playing the Red Foxes, a scrawny but smug group of kids from a town over. Their pitcher tosses the ball into his mitt. He's a short, pale white kid with big ears. A bridge of freckles wrinkles across his nose when he sniffs.

I *should* be cheering Tyler on. Don't get me wrong. I want to win the game, but I also wouldn't *hate* it if Tyler—

SMACK!

Aaaaand he smashes the first pitch straight into left field. Of course.

The shortstop stretches for the ball, but it shoots past him. It rolls into the grass, and the left fielder chases after it. Meanwhile, Tyler explodes from home plate, chucking his bat to the ground with a *thump*. He makes it all the way to second base.

I glance over my shoulder. Mr. Sudbury's at the chain-link fence, fist pumping the air. Dad steps behind him and claps him on the shoulder, congratulating him. Then he winks at me.

I spin back around to the field. My legs shake. That wink was supposed to feel like a high five, like a "you got this!" but what if I don't got this?

Omar presses his shoulder into mine. "Hey," he says.

Every inch of me starts to sweat. I don't want to look at him. If I do, he'll see how nervous I am. I'm so embarrassing. But I say back, "What?"

"It's okay," he whispers. "I get nervous too."

I look at him now. He's Black with light brown skin. His inky black hair is cut close to his scalp in sharp, even lines. He's smiling like he cares. The little gap between his front teeth is showing. It's a nice gap. "But you're *really* good," I say. "You've *always* been good."

He shrugs. "That doesn't make it any easier."

Coach Mathis pokes his head around the fence and nods at us. "Jones, you're up."

Omar exhales through his nose. "Wish me luck."

"Okay," I say. "But you don't really need it."

He snorts. "We'll see."

I worry I said the wrong thing. That I offended him or something. Why is this so hard? We used to get each other. I miss that. I miss *him*. So far, the best thing about being a Blue Whale is hanging out with him. I just wish we could go back to how we were. Without the team. And that it had never come between us.

He practice swings over home plate, fingers flexing on the grip.

I stand up to cheer him on. "Knock it out of the park, Omar!"

He doesn't look back. That kind of stings.

The first pitch is a ball, which means it was thrown too far outside the strike zone. Omar swings for the second but misses. On the third pitch he makes contact—a line drive. The second baseman grabs the ball and hurls it to first. He catches it a millisecond after Omar runs through.

"SAFE," the umpire calls.

"All right, all right!" Tyler shouts, dancing on third.

I didn't realize I'd been holding my breath. I let out a quiet sigh. He did it. Just like I knew he would. And if he can, maybe I can too.

"You ready, Lorenzini?" Coach Mathis asks. He's tall, white, and old enough to be my grandpa. He rests his clipboard on his potbelly shelf.

"Absolutely," I say, which is only half-true.

My toes tingle. I squeeze them in my shoes, which feel snug all of a sudden. Sometimes when I get anxious, things feel too close, too tight. I flex, then clench my toes, but the sensation won't go away. I ignore my nerves best I can and grab my aluminum bat. They aren't getting the best of me. Not today. I march to home plate, determined to crush this.

Behind me, Dad shouts, "Keep your eye on the ball!"

"You've got this, baby!" Mom adds.

I can't look back at them. It'll only make me more nervous. Focus on hitting the ball. Just like Omar did. At the thought of him, I can't help glancing his way. To my surprise, he gives me a thumbs-up.

Fireflies light in my chest. Out of everyone here, I'm a little surprised he's the one who makes me feel like I can do this. Like there's an actual chance I'll get a hit and make it to first. Which is weird since I don't even know if we're really friends again. He's probably just being a good teammate.

"Come on," Tyler shouts. "Get me home, Matty!"

Ugh. I hate when people call me that, which Tyler knows. We've been in the same class since third grade. He's always called me everything *but* Matteo.

"Remember the grip!" Dad hollers.

"Get us a run!" Coach Mathis yells, hands pressed to the sides of his mouth like a megaphone.

The fireflies dim. Pressure fills my lungs. *What if I can't get us a run?* I spin the bat in my hands. Dad's expecting me to be like Tyler. Like Omar. Failure isn't an option. I can't look weak. Not in front of my parents or Coach or Tyler. And definitely not Omar.

There's no other option. I've gotta man up and do this.

But my mind speeds around in dizzy circles as the pitcher hikes up his leg. I ready the bat, but the tornado in my brain won't let up. I can't focus. The pitcher's arm shoots forward. The ball torpedoes at me. And I freeze.

"Strike one!" the umpire shouts.

"Aw, come on!" Tyler cries. He's lunging forward from third, one foot barely touching the base, poised to run.

Just hit the ball, Matteo, I tell myself. *That's all you've gotta do.*

Hit. The. Ball.

I breathe out, then in. Cool air prickles my throat.

The pitcher winds up again and hurls the ball. But something's wrong. It's coming in too close. Everything is too close all of a sudden. I flinch, sure it's going to hit me, and the umpire calls, "Strike two!"

"That's all right, Matteo," Dad yells. "Hang in there."

"This next one's yours," says Mom.

I'm not so sure about that. I dare another look at Tyler, who's scowling. His face says, *Don't mess this up.* Other guys, like Freddie McCoy, are shouting at me to hit the ball. *Just hit it!* Maybe they're trying to give me a boost, but all I feel is pressure. It pinches at my shoulders and weighs down my stomach.

I shake the stress off best I can and stamp my feet into the ground. I've gotta do this for Dad. I choke up on the bat. *You can do it,* I tell myself, even though it feels like a lie.

The crowd quiets. The pitcher's arm pulls back, and he releases a lightning pitch. It flies at me, faster, faster, faster. Everything inside me seizes up. I swing—

FUMP.

"Ow!" The ball collides with my shoulder. Hard. My eyes sting. I blink hard and fast, trying not to cry, but that only makes tears roll down my face. My cheeks light with embarrassment. *Man up, Matteo.* I swipe away the wet streaks.

Coach Mathis is suddenly at my side. "You okay, kid?"

I nod. "It actually doesn't hurt that bad." Which is true. And weird.

"You sure?" Coach asks. "That pitch had some heat to it."

"I'm stronger than I look," I say.

Coach still looks unconvinced, and now I feel weird for not hurting more. I seriously can't win.

"Take your base," the umpire calls.

I do, putting on the bravest face I can. The crowd claps politely, as if I did something other than get hit. Omar walks to second, but Tyler's got to stay on third. I steal a glance at the other Blue Whales. The guys in the dugout are already cheering on Freddie McCoy, who's up to bat next. Omar smiles at me quickly but then focuses his sights on third.

Tyler, though. He makes sure I see the annoyance in his eyes. He shakes his head at me like I'm a total waste of space.

. . . .

MILES SUDBURY

Oh, yeah, sure. I played baseball as a kid. But my son, Tyler, well, he's a real pro. Got an arm on him like a cannon.

MATTEO LORENZINI

Was baseball a big part of your life growing up in Creekside?

MILES SUDBURY

Sure, I guess. Kept me fit. Most kids these days, they don't stay active the way they should. Cell phones and video games. Boys gotta be active. Do hard stuff. Testing the limits of your body and mind—that's what makes a boy a man. You're on your way, aren't you, Matty?

MATTEO LORENZINI

It's Matteo.

FOUR

We lose the game, seven to six. It isn't my fault, but Tyler sure makes me feel like it is. I overhear him whisper to Freddie, "If he could just hit the freaking ball." I can't look the other Blue Whales in the eye after that, not even Omar. My face burns so hot I almost light on fire.

Soon as the game is over, I grab my things and beeline for home. Nice thing about small town living is that everything's in walking distance, which means I can make a quick escape. Mom and Dad have to jog to catch up with me at the edge of the field.

"Sport, hey!" Dad calls. "Wait up."

I slow my pace, but only a little. "What?"

They huff on either side of me. Mom pulls me to her, but I squirm away. "Not in front of the guys," I say. Babying me will only make everything worse.

"Let me see your arm," Dad says, reaching for my sleeve. "That looked painful."

"It's fine. I mean, it hurts a little, but I—I just want to go home."

Dad tips his head toward downtown. "Why don't we stop for some ice cream first? A little chocolate chip cookie dough usually fixed me right up after a tough game."

I shake my head. "No thanks."

"Aw, c'mon."

I turn toward home. "Not in the mood."

Dad cracks his knuckles. "Matteo Lorenzini, I challenge you to a fireman's race."

Mom mock gasps. "Oh snap."

I slow my roll. A "fireman's race" is our term for an eating competition. The name comes from when Dad's at the firehouse and they get a call, and he's got to gobble down his food on his way to an emergency. I grin. Maybe a little ice cream wouldn't hurt.

"You're on." I shove my gear into Dad's arms and blast off, shouting, "First one to Conehead's gets a head start!"

Dad's feet pound the pavement behind me. "Get back here, you little cheat!" he shouts, laughing.

I beat Dad to Conehead's by a millisecond. We huff through the doorway of the ice cream parlor, while Mom takes her sweet time coming down the sidewalk behind us. Mrs. Curtis, the store owner, greets us from behind the counter. She's Black and has dark brown skin, so smooth and glossy the sun shines brightly on her raised cheekbones.

Her mint-green apron is smudged by swaths of strawberry and chocolate ice cream stains. "Well, if it isn't my favorite customers," she says, which I'm pretty sure she says to everyone. "What can I do you for?"

I lace my fingers together and rest my hands on the counter, all business. "Two vanilla cones, please. Extra, *extra* tall."

Her fingernails clack on the register, and then she heads to the stack of waffle cones behind her. "Y'all doing one of those fire drills or whatever you call them?"

"Fireman's *race*," I say. "I'm gonna get him this time."

Dad takes out his wallet. "Okay, Mr. Confident." He hands his credit card to Mrs. Curtis. "How's your day been, Liz?"

She slides his card into the reader. "Slow start. You're my first customers of the day. Here you go." She gives Dad back his card, and then we watch while she fills our cones. We're practically drooling by the time she hands us each an ivory tower of swirled soft serve. Dad and I tiptoe to one of the tabletops, careful not to let them topple. Just as Mom *dings* through the doorway, I dive in, having earned my head start from the race. I chomp off a huge glob and swallow it whole. My esophagus burns with cold.

Dad counts down my head start and then attacks his cone. He slurps off the whole top of his twist, downing it in a single gulp. He's not messing around today, but there's no way I am letting him win. I gobble faster.

Disaster strikes when I'm halfway down my spiral. Sharp pain pierces my forehead. "Brain freeze!" I shout, pressing my thumb against the roof of my mouth. "Ow, ow, ow!"

Dad chuckles. He's been rapid-fire licking away, and he's nearly down to the cone. "That'll teach you. Slow and steady wins the race."

When the pain finally lessens, I drag my saliva-ed thumb on my pants. I'll show him. I jab my finger at the shop window. "What's that?"

Dad spins around and I smash my cone on top of his, lopping off my remaining ice cream so he's restacked and I'm down to just the cone.

"You little sneak!" he shouts, whipping back around.

I gnash into my cone, while Dad speed licks his extra ice cream.

I've got him this time.

Mom chuckles, wagging her head at us like we're ridiculous. She leans over the counter to Mrs. Curtis. "Sometimes it's like I have *two* sons."

"I know that life," she agrees. "My Darius was the biggest child out of all our kids."

I stuff the tip of the cone into my mouth, cheeks bulging like a chipmunk's, and shout, "DONE!" My fist rises in the air victoriously as I parade around the shop. Mom and Mrs. Curtis golf clap. I bow to my adoring fans.

Dad's eyebrows furrow and he wags his half-eaten cone

at me. "All right, punk. Looks like the better fireman won today. But no cheating next time." He winks.

Not missing a beat, I say, "I don't know what you're talking about."

When we get home, I head to my room, close the door, and starfish backward on my bed. I'm wiped out and stuffed with ice cream.

"Well, Cricket," I say, tilting my chin in the direction of his bowl. "I might not be able to hit a baseball, but I can eat an ice cream cone."

He blows a bubble.

"You're right. I *should* be proud."

Cricket's glazed eyes stare into the distance. I sit up and unlace my shoes. Something crunches inside. Gravel? Dirt? My feet *have* felt weird ever since I got up to bat. I kick off one shoe, then the other. Then I peel back my right sock.

That's weird. Crushed-up leaves—brown and green and gold—cling to the fuzzy fabric and crumble to my bedroom floor. My foot is nasty sweaty. Bits of leaf stick to my skin. I wipe my foot clean with my comforter. Then I take off my left sock and find more leaf bits.

"Cricket, you saw me get ready this morning. Did I put on dirty socks?" I examine the leaf flecks confetti-ing my floor. "*I don't think so*," I mumble in my best Cricket impression. "*But with you, I'd be-*leaf *anything.*"

Feet shuffle behind my door. "Matteo?"

I kick the leaf bits under my dirty baseball clothes as Dad walks into the room. My parents get angry when I bring the outside in, and I have a bad habit of walking around the yard barefoot or in my socks and making a mess of things. "What's up?" I say.

Fortunately, Dad doesn't seem to notice. "I know ice cream can turn a frown upside down, but I wanted to check in on you." He sits on the bed next to me. "That wasn't an easy first game, but we'll keep practicing. You'll do better next time."

Better next time. The game. Of course. I kind of hoped we were done with that for today. "I don't really want to talk about it right now."

But he goes on, "Did you see how Omar—how he sort of positioned himself when the ball was coming at him?"

I want to melt into my bedsheets. He *has* to bring up Omar of all people. "Yeah, Dad. He's perfect. I *know*."

Omar's perfect. I know what I meant by that but hearing myself say it makes my armpits sweat. I picture him giving me a thumbs-up earlier, and my stomach trampolines.

Dad shakes his head. "That's not what I'm saying. But you can learn from each other. That's what makes a great team."

My gaze falls to my dirty uniform on the floor. "What if you only need help? What if you have nothing else to offer?"

"Matteo, look at me." He grabs me by the shoulders. "You have tons to offer. Don't let one game get you down."

What if it's not just this game? I think. But I say, "Sure. Whatever."

"Why don't you take a shower?" Dad says. "You'll feel better washing away the grime." His eyes drift to my comforter and the bits of leaf all over it. He points at the mess and says, "Tracked a whole bunch of nature back in with you again. Clean this up before your mom sees?"

I flush. "Yeah, I'll take care of it."

He winks. "I know you will. You're Matteo Lorenzini! You can take care of anything."

SUBJECT: MAYOR MEYERS

. . . .

MATTEO LORENZINI

What else can you tell us about the tree?

MAYOR MEYERS

Fun fact: Did you know that no matter where you stand in downtown Creekside, you can always see the topmost branches? Take a look out the window. You see?

MATTEO LORENZINI

It's like it's watching us.

FIVE

Okay, so maybe Dad knows what he's talking about because I feel a little better after a shower. At least until I towel off and my reflection reminds me how scrawny I am. My arms are seriously skinnier than spaghetti. I'm like a toddler in comparison to Tyler or Omar. I don't get what's wrong with me. Why isn't my body doing what it's supposed to? At this rate, I'll always be Mom and Dad's miracle baby, with an emphasis on *baby*.

My parents are talking in the living room when I come down. Dad whistles at me. "Lookin' like a million bucks. How's your arm?"

"Sore, but it's fine."

"You sure?" He lifts my T-shirt sleeve and rubs his thumb over my arm where the ball hit. I try not to wince and fail. He frowns. "Looks a little discolored. Maybe we should have Dr. Wilson take a look?"

Mom clucks at him. "Oh, Vin. Boys are built for bruises. He's fine."

The doorbell rings before they can debate any further. Dad moves for the door, and his voice booms from the hall a second later. "Matteo, it's for you."

I don't have a chance to respond before Azura Gonzalez, my next-door neighbor and best friend, barges into the room. Her long, wavy blue hair is unbrushed and wind-blown over her shoulders. Her amber skin glows pink from the brisk spring air. She's wearing a green sweater and dark jeans. She's already kicked off her shoes, revealing purple fuzzy socks. In her hands is a white box, which she thrusts at me so that her arms are free to circle my shoulders.

"I heard about the game," she says. "Are you okay?"

"What?" I pull away, a little nervous. "How do *you* know what happened?" My stomach drops. "Are people talking about me?"

"No, no. I called her," Mom says quickly. "Thought you could use some friend time."

Azura points to the box. "I brought brownies. They make everything better."

Her dad, Sergio Gonzalez, owns Creekside Bakery down the street. It's been in their family forever. And Mr. Gonzalez makes the *best* brownies. Even though I just downed a whole bunch of ice cream, my mouth waters. The base of the box is warm, which means they're fresh.

"Thanks. They smell amazing," I say.

As much as I wish Mom had run it by me before calling Azura, I'm glad she did. Being an only child is a lot sometimes. A lot of *attention*. A lot of *time*. A lot of *energy*. Tack on my "miracle kid" status and I'm pretty much drowning in expectations. Sometimes I need a break from being the center of everything. When Azura's here, I can breathe for a minute.

"We're gonna get dinner started," says Dad. "You two can hang out in here, okay?"

Mom points to the box. "I'll bring some milk for those."

"Thanks, Mrs. L," says Azura. Then she swings her legs onto the couch. "Tell me everything."

"I don't know," I say. "It's not that big a deal. I was nervous and choked. That's it. End of story."

She pokes my arm. "Does it hurt?"

"Ow. A little!" I open the box and pull out a brownie.

She lifts my shirtsleeve. Her fingers are cold on my skin. "It *looks* fine. Maybe a little yellow. The way your dad was talking in the background when your mom called, it sounded like you needed a whole new arm." She laughs.

"They always make things seem worse than they are," I say through a mouthful of insanely delicious, fudgy brownie.

She grins, her eyes narrowing. "Now for the real question." She scoots closer and whispers, "How were things with Omar?"

My legs squirm, but I try to keep my tone even. "Fine, I guess?"

"So he's friends with you again? Just like that? No apology or anything? What about—"

Mom walks in with two glasses of milk, saving me from the storm of Omar questions. She sets them on the coffee table and nods at Azura. "Any funny videos for us?"

Azura fumbles for a second, clearly still on Omar. But she pulls out her cell phone, something I'm still not allowed to have, which totally sucks, and says, "Have I shown you the squirrel one? Where it fights a balloon? Derek Jones, Omar's brother, posted it a few days ago."

Mom's face wrinkles a little at the mention of Omar's name, but she holds out her hand. "Let me see."

Azura gives her the phone. Mom watches, snort-laughing halfway through the video. This always happens. Even when I have *my* friend over, Mom or Dad finds a way to cut in. It's like they can't help themselves. Finally, Mom hands it back, chuckling. "Didn't expect that ending! All right, I'll let you two get back to it." She disappears back into the kitchen, though I'm sure she'll somehow end up butting in again soon. She always does.

I gulp down some milk and seize the opportunity to shift the conversation away from Omar. "I forgot to check. Are you good for Dorothy Van Otten on Monday?"

This past fall, Azura got the idea to film a documentary about Creekside to celebrate the two-hundred-year anniversary of the town's founding after Ms. Grainger, our social studies teacher, showed us this docuseries about small towns of the Midwest. Azura became totally obsessed with launching herself into stardom by making something just like it, and I (mostly happily) got roped into filming it with her. Lately, I've taken on setting up interviews while she edits the video clips. And it's actually been pretty fun. We're on track to finish it before the bicentennial celebration, but only just.

"Totally," Azura says. "Camera's charged and ready to go."

"Awesome. Be prepared though. She was a little *strange* on the phone."

Azura helps herself to a brownie. "Really? Dad was just talking about her. Says she has some pretty interesting stories."

I snort. "Probably all about cats. I heard she's got like seventeen of them!"

She giggles and waggles are eyebrows. "*Purrrr*obably."

I laugh too. But the more we talk about the interview, the more I think about Monday. About school. A knot pulls tighter in my gut. "I wish I could skip school and jump right to the interview. Did I tell you I heard Tyler talking about me to Freddie?"

Azura groans. "Ugh. TYLER. We *loathe* Tyler. Ignore him. You didn't hit the ball? So what. Not a big deal." She grabs her glass of milk, grinning evilly. "Remember that time Stevie Price peed his pants in first grade? *That* was embarrassing."

"Oh my god," I laugh. "I totally forgot about that."

Azura's right. Maybe there are worse things to be embarrassed about.

CREEKSIDE DOCUMENTARY TRANSCRIPT #5

SUBJECT: NANCY MANDRAKE

. . . .

NANCY MANDRAKE

I took this teaching position precisely because it was in Creek-side. I've always loved it here. My family used to visit when I was a kid. We always had to make a stop at the bakery.

AZURA GONZALEZ

For real? You know that's my family's bakery, right?

NANCY MANDRAKE

I pieced that together, but I didn't want to fangirl too much.

AZURA GONZALEZ

Well, if you ever do want to fangirl, my dad's very single and lookin' to mingle.

NANCY MANDRAKE

(Laughs) Darling, I'm married. Flattered but married.

SIX

I pretend to be sick Monday morning, but Mom isn't buying it. As a last resort, I tell her I'm nervous about what kids might say about me flopping at Saturday's game and that's why I don't want to go. That majorly backfires. "You're not missing school," she says. "But I did email your teachers and your counselor to let them know you might be feeling anxious. They'll keep an eye out for you." She hands me my lunch in a brown paper bag. "And don't forget we've got an appointment with Dr. Wilson after school today."

A multicolored welt bloomed on my arm yesterday. I don't want to admit it, but it hurts pretty bad now. But Mom's right—I *should* be able to handle a bruise. "I don't know why we have to go," I say. "I'm fine. And Azura and I have an interview."

"I don't disagree, but the interview will have to wait," she says. "Your dad insists. It's for his peace of mind more than anything. You know how he gets. Now don't be late."

Frustrated, I catch up to Azura at the end of the block, and together we walk the rest of the way to school. "My parents are making me go to the doctor this afternoon," I say, showing off the bruise on my arm. "Is it okay if we reschedule filming with Dorothy? I don't want to miss anything."

"Sure," says Azura. "I can work on more edits today instead!"

I brighten. "Awesome. I'll give her a call later."

We round the corner and Creekside Middle School comes into view. My shoulders tense. Tyler Sudbury and Freddie McCoy are kicking rocks at the flagpole outside the main entrance.

"Tyler's totally going to make fun of me," I say. "They all will."

"They won't," says Azura. "It was just a game. And they've got the attention span of goldfish—no offense to goldfish, LOL. But if they do, they'll hear from me."

"Oh yeah? *You're* going to stand up to Tyler?"

She waves her hand at the mention of his name. "He's a twerp."

"He's a foot taller than you!"

"Well, I *feel* taller than him."

Wish I could say the same. But deep down, if I'm being honest, I'm not *really* worried about what Tyler thinks. Or Freddie. I pick at a hangnail on my left pinky. "What if Omar stops talking to me again? Like he thought we could be friends again and then he saw me play and was like, 'Nope!'"

She side-eyes me. "You need to get out of your head."

Despite her reassurances, I get a couple of weird looks as we walk in the double doors. While I'm at my locker, Lillian Vosticzek whispers something to Jennie O'Connor and they both start laughing. Azura says they probably weren't even talking about me. ("Those two are always snorting about something.") I'm not sure that makes me feel much better.

I get to first period without drawing too much attention to myself, but Mrs. Mandrake pats my desk like every two minutes and gives me the *are you okay?* eyes. I nod so much in those first forty-five minutes I might as well be a bobblehead. I wish Mom hadn't emailed half the school about me. This is my fault. I shouldn't have made such a big deal about everything this morning.

But by lunch, it seems like most kids have gotten bored talking about me, if they even were. I sit with Azura at our usual table, eating the turkey sandwich Mom packed me. On the napkin she sent, there's a note in her handwriting: *I love you to the moon and back. —Mom.* Her notes always make me smile, but I crumple it quick when someone new joins our table.

It's Omar Jones.

He takes the seat across from me, next to Azura, and I instantly start sweating. He hasn't sat with us all school year. After he made the Blue Whales and I didn't last spring, he slowly disappeared from my life. Then I didn't hear from him all summer, which made me sad, then angry, then sad again. When this school year started, it was like I didn't even exist. He's been friendly since I made the team, but nothing like this. What the what?

"Hey," he says. He's in a gray hoodie. The string that should be in the hood is missing. "Mind if I sit with you guys?"

I nod, all ability to form words gone. Does this mean he's *not* embarrassed by me?

Azura's eyes flash my way, but she says, as if this isn't totally weird, "Yeah. What do you have today?"

He shows off his tray. "School lunch. Mashed potatoes and . . . meat loaf?" He pokes at something orange. "I think these are supposed to be carrots." He shoves them to one side of his Styrofoam plate.

Azura makes a *blech* face and holds out a muffin. "I've got an extra. You want it?"

His eyes widen. "Is that one of your dad's?"

"Obviously."

"Then one hundred percent yes," he says. "Thanks."

He pulls off the muffin top and eats it like a cookie. His face melts into a grin. I wait for the dimple to show up. When it does, I melt a little. But then he catches me looking and I laser focus on my turkey sandwich. Buttery warmth fizzles in my chest. *Get it together, Matteo!*

"I've been thinking about you since the game," he says.

Here it is. The reason he's here. I'm sure he's gonna tell me all the ways I could have hit the ball, or worse—that I should quit the team. I wish I could be the turkey hiding between the bread in my hands. "I should have hit it," I mumble, my voice dropping.

"What?" He licks his fingers. "No way. That was a crap pitch. You couldn't hit that."

I sit up a little taller, surprised. But I say, "*You* could have."

"Yeah right," he laughs. "I mean, I probably would have *dodged* it at least. Sounded like it hurt! You're tougher than you look."

I grin at the sort-of compliment. Maybe this isn't going so bad. "Thanks?"

Then I look to Azura, who's been watching all this while nibbling apple slices. She's the only person who knows I have complicated *feelings* about Omar, which I honestly didn't know I had until he stopped being my friend. Once he was gone, I started realizing how I really felt about him. At first, I missed him, and then I *really* missed him. So much my stomach hurt. But then it wasn't just my stomach—it was my heart too. Both of which are battling each other inside my chest at this very moment. And now he must have seen me look at her because he says, "What? Did I say something? Do I have muffin on my face?"

"No, no. It's nothing," I say. "You're fine."

Then another lunch tray crashes onto the table. Tyler Sudbury looms over me. Freddie McCoy stands behind him. He looks like he's holding back a fit of laughter. Tyler says, "You know you're supposed to hit the ball with the bat, not your arm, right?"

I swallow, not looking up. My insides squirm.

"Oh, come on. Leave him alone," says Omar.

Tyler leans over my chips, ignoring him. "We'll have 'em throw real slow for you next time. Maybe you'll hit it then."

In my mind I'm sliding right under the table. I don't want to answer. Azura opens her mouth like she's gonna lash out, but to my surprise, Omar beats her to it. "I said lay off him, man."

"I'm just saying!" Tyler holds up his hands like he's innocent. "Maybe you should go back to T-ball, Matty. You'd kill it with the four-year-olds."

Freddie snickers. My leg twitches under the table.

"Get out of here, Tyler," Azura says, "or I'll get one of the lunch monitors."

Tyler chuckles. "You would. Go ahead. See if I care."

"Leave." Azura stands. "Now."

Tyler lifts his tray from the table. "Whatever."

When he's gone, Azura and Omar fume, mumbling to each other about what a jerk Tyler is, but I don't say anything. All I want to do is run away. Finally making the team was supposed to make my life better. But nothing I ever do is enough for me to fit in. Heat creeps all over my skin. I'm sure the whole cafeteria is staring. The pressure behind my eyes is building, and I can't afford to look weaker than I already do. So I pick up my tray and dash for the doors, ignoring Azura and Omar when they call after me.

CREEKSIDE DOCUMENTARY TRANSCRIPT #6

SUBJECT: LILLIAN VOSTICZEK

· ·

AZURA GONZALEZ

What are some of your earliest Creekside memories?

LILLIAN VOSTICZEK

How early?

AZURA GONZALEZ

Like, when you were a kid.

LILLIAN VOSTICZEK

We are kids.

AZURA GONZALEZ

You know what I mean.

LILLIAN VOSTICZEK

*Um, let me think. (Closes eyes) I remember moving in. It
was raining. I was four. Mr. Kowalski—he's our next-door
neighbor—he read to me under a yellow umbrella all morning
while my parents hauled boxes. I didn't want to be inside without them. I was too scared. (Smiles) Mr. Kowalski's the best.*

SEVEN

The library is the oldest part of Creekside Middle School. Mom says back when the building was a one-room schoolhouse, the library was all there was. Over the years, the floors were redone and the shelves replaced, but there's an old *feeling* in this part of the school that I love. These walls are safe. Sturdy. Dust motes play in the afternoon sun streaming through the windows. I breathe in the bookish smell, shoving Tyler out of my mind.

A grumbly voice greets me. "Matteo, what are you doing here?"

Mr. Kowalski, the elderly librarian, shuffles forward, his bony hand clutching the top of his wooden cane. He's wispy and tall with waxy white skin and a tuft of cirrus hair that shapeshifts on his head just like a cloud. He's wearing a gray sweater vest over a blue collared shirt and khaki pants. His lanyard *fwaps* against his chest as he walks.

"Hi, Mr. Kowalski," I say, hoping he doesn't ask for a hall

pass. "I needed to leave the cafeteria."

His gray-white caterpillar brows scrunch behind his glasses. "You didn't get into trouble, did you?"

"Oh. No, nothing like that," I say quickly.

"Hmm." He clears his throat. "Are you doing okay?"

"I'll be fine."

The cane centers in front of the old man, both of his hands coming to rest on top of it. I can't read his expression, but he watches me intently. He finally says, "Would you like to sit here awhile?"

I look around. Aside from us, the library is empty. Empty is good. "Sure," I say.

"Excellent!" He brightens, turning to the circulation desk. "You can help me check in these books."

A skyscraper of novels teeters next to a barcode scanner and computer screen. I internally groan. Mr. Kowalski *would* put me to work. Maybe I shouldn't have come here.

"I'll open to the barcode," he says, resting his cane against the counter. "And you can scan them in. How does that sound?"

"Yeah." I nod. "I can do that."

There's a rhythm to the work, almost like music. Flip, shove, scan, close. Flip, shove, scan, close. I slip into the pattern of it, working faster and faster. Flip, shove, scan, close. Mr. Kowalski is pretty quick for an old guy.

"Lorenzini . . . you know," Mr. Kowalski muses, sliding

over another book. "I was the librarian here when your dad was a kid." He huffs on his glasses and smooths away the fog. "I grew up with your grandfather too. You remind me of him. Your father too. There's a certain Lorenzini charm, I suppose."

Now he's got my full attention. No one ever mentions Grandpa. I'm intrigued, but I say, "Oh. I'm adopted."

Mr. Kowalski shrugs. "We inherit all sorts of things from our families, not all of them biological." He smiles. "You have their same quiet way about you when you're upset."

Embarrassed that I'm so obvious, I stare down, my shoe scuffing the floor.

He goes on. "I remember your dad coming in one day after a PE class. Very upset. Scraped knee. He helped me check in books that day too." Mr. Kowalski pats the screen. "But computers looked a *little* different in those days."

The old man seems to lose himself to a memory. When he doesn't go on, I can't help but ask, "So, um, what was wrong with him?"

"Who?"

"My dad."

"Oh!" Mr. Kowalski chuckles to himself. "Real tough guy, that Vinny. Told me he was fine, but"—he taps next to his eyes—"I saw the truth."

I scan another book. "Did you find out what was wrong with him?"

"Eventually." He slides a tattered paperback down.

When he doesn't go on, I say, "So . . . what *was* wrong?"

"Nothing talking it out couldn't help."

I roll my eyes at the screen. Now I see what he's up to. I take another book from him, saying, "I'm not my dad."

"Sure," he says, "but the same medicine works on most of us." Mr. Kowalski doesn't hand me another book, but he does look at me expectantly over the top of his glasses.

I groan. "Fiiine." I take a deep breath before saying, "There's a kid who keeps making fun of me. Because I suck at baseball." I pause because that's only half-true and decide to add, "He makes me feel like I suck at *everything*."

"Why is that?"

"No matter what I do, I'm just not good enough. I've been trying. *Really* hard. All Dad and I've been doing lately is batting practice. Even Coach said I was looking better at our last team practice, but our first game this past weekend . . . it was *bad*. I couldn't even hit the ball. And all Lorenzinis are supposed to play baseball. It's like a *thing* in our family." I meet Mr. Kowalski's gaze. "I love baseball, but I guess I didn't inherit *that* family talent."

He scratches his nose. "Talent shmalent. Seems to me you got what really matters: a heart."

I roll my eyes. "Can't use a heart to play baseball."

"Perhaps not." Mr. Kowalski opens another book. "But it's useful for so much more."

"I don't want to do more," I say. "I want to be good at baseball. I want to be like the other guys."

"*There's* your problem."

"What?"

"Wanting to be like everyone else," he says. "You'll be much happier if you strive to be *you*. You're the only thing you have, and *you* are special just the way you are." He sniffs. "Wish someone had told *me* that earlier in my life."

I sigh. "I'm not, though. I'm just one giant flop of a human being."

Mr. Kowalski's tone grows stern. "Matteo Lorenzini, you are not a flop. Don't let other people keep you from seeing the truth. Easier said than done, I know, but—"

Brrriiiiiing! The end of fifth period bell rings.

"Eh, time to move on," Mr. Kowalski says.

"Do I have to?" I ask.

He smiles. "Yes. Yes, you do."

"Fiiine."

I walk around the circulation counter and out of the library. I swim upstream against the shoulders of my classmates, and I realize that I'm not as frustrated as I was before. Maybe Mr. Kowalski was right. It did feel kind of good to get some of that off my chest.

CREEKSIDE DOCUMENTARY TRANSCRIPT #7

SUBJECT: JENNIE O'CONNOR

. . . .

MATTEO LORENZINI

What about you? What's your earliest Creekside memory?

JENNIE O'CONNOR

I only moved here last year, so I guess the day I moved in too.

MATTEO LORENZINI

What was the first thing you noticed about Creekside?

JENNIE O'CONNOR

How obsessed everyone is with Creekside! (Laughs) You guys, like, really love your town. It's weird.

EIGHT

Dr. Wilson presses her stethoscope to my chest. "Not too cold, is it?"

I shake my head. Dr. Wilson is an older white woman with hair that used to be inky black but is now salted with gray. She has a wide face and a big smile filled with coffee-stained teeth, but her breath always smells minty.

"Good news," she says, pulling the stethoscope away.

"What?" I ask.

She raps my knee with her knuckles. "You've got a beating heart and healthy lungs."

Mom stops picking at her cuticles. "But what about his arm? That's why we came."

I lift the sleeve on my T-shirt and poke at the bruised flesh. "It hurts when I do this."

"Then you shouldn't do that." Dr. Wilson chuckles. Then she adjusts her glasses on her nose and zeros in on my arm. She pokes above my elbow, into my nonexistent bicep, and then my slumped shoulder, asking each time if it hurts. It does, a little. She raises my arm and checks the underside. Then she moves to my right arm and conducts the same inspection. All the while she's quiet except for her tongue, which clicks every so often. I try not to worry about what those clicks mean.

At last, she says, "Aside from the bruising, your arm looks perfectly fine to me. Nothing's broken or sprained. It'll be sore for a few days." She looks me in the eye. "Far as I can tell, you are a completely normal, healthy eleven-year-old boy."

Mom crosses her legs and smiles. "Well, that's a relief."

"The other guys my age, though," I say, seizing the opportunity to figure out what I really what to know. "They're all getting bigger. Stronger. When will I?"

Dr. Wilson hangs the stethoscope around her neck. "You'll sprout right up any day now. If you're anything like your da—" She stops herself, and I cringe. She was probably going to say, *If you're anything like your dad.* Most of the time I let comments like that roll off, but after all that inherited talent talk with Mr. Kowalski today, it hits a little harder. She fidgets with the stethoscope. "Just be patient. You want arms thick as tree trunks, I'm sure you'll get 'em soon enough."

"But when?" I ask.

"When the time's right," she says. She turns to Mom. "I'll have the nurse bring in your paperwork. If the bruising gets worse or the pain increases, give us a call, okay?"

"Thank you, Dr. Wilson," says Mom.

"Thanks," I mumble.

The door *clicks* closed on her way out. Mom leans forward and places a hand on my knee. "Dr. Wilson, she didn't mean—"

"It's fine," I say.

A silent moment passes. Then Mom says, "I didn't know you were feeling so insecure about your body."

I shrug. "I'm—I was just curious."

She squeezes my leg. "Okay, well, I'll text your dad. He'll want an update. He was worried you might have to sit out a game. He'll be thrilled."

Yeah, I think. *Until he sees that I'm still just me. Not Tyler. Not Omar.*

Just Matteo.

CREEKSIDE DOCUMENTARY TRANSCRIPT #8

SUBJECT: STEVIE PRICE

. . . .

STEVIE PRICE

This isn't about me peeing my pants, is it?

AZURA GONZALEZ

Do you want it to be about you peeing your pants?

STEVIE PRICE

What do you think?

AZURA GONZALEZ

I mean, you brought it up.

STEVIE PRICE

*I was six! I couldn't help it! Is this all I'll ever be known for?
Is this my life? I WON'T LET THIS DEFINE ME.*

AZURA GONZALEZ

Um, thanks for your time, Stevie.

NINE

After school the next day, I follow Azura through downtown Creekside. It rained earlier, and even though it's sunny now, the grass is damp and the air smells like wet leaves. I love spring. Flowers blooming, trees budding. Chirping baby birds calling out from newly woven nests. Even the earthworms, strung along the sidewalk like fat noodles.

But I can't stop thinking about what Dr. Wilson said yesterday. How I'm "a healthy, normal boy," even though it feels like I'll never catch up with the other guys. When *do* I get to be a real boy? When's it my turn?

To make matters worse, Tyler hasn't let up his teasing. And Omar looks at me like I'm a puppy in a cone whenever baseball gets brought up. (He sat with Tyler and the other guys instead of me and Azura at lunch today, but he *did* say hi to me in the hall, so that's something.)

"Come on," Azura says, snapping me out of my thoughts.

"We're going to be late. You told her we'd be there by three thirty, right?"

"Yeah." I look over my shoulder at the clock tower above the mayor's office. "We have two whole minutes."

"A good documentarian is never late." She turns down Hester Street, making for an old brick building. Flannery's Flower Shop is on the first floor with apartments above it. "Was she okay with us rescheduling?"

"Totally," I say. "Said that gave her more time to bake cookies for us!"

Azura gives me a *told ya so* face. "See? She's not strange. She's sweet!"

Azura's seen the best in people as long as I've known her, which is pretty much my whole life. Mom says we were in diapers together (not the same ones). That's probably why we make such a great team. She presses the buzzer for apartment four. "It's Azura Gonzalez and Matteo Lorenzini," she says into the speaker.

There's no response, but the door buzzes and the lock clicks. Azura pulls me inside, and I follow her up the narrow staircase, one, two, three flights, until we get to apartment four. Even though it's the end of March, there's a worn mat at the door that says "Merry Christmas." On Azura's third knock, the door swings open.

Dorothy Van Otten's hair is tightly curled and paper

white. Tortoiseshell glasses on a beaded chain hang around her neck. Her milky skin is age-spotted, especially along her arms. Her black turtleneck is covered in cat hair, and her plaid pants would make great wallpaper in an old home. An enormous white cat glares at us from her arms, its tail wagging at her elbow. From behind her wafts an overwhelming stench of litter box mixed with cinnamon sugar. My nose wrinkles. It's an unsettling combination.

"Oh, dearies! I'm so glad you came," she says. "Come in, come in!"

"Thank you for meeting with us today," says Azura. "Sorry we had to reschedule."

"Of course! No problem at all. I know both your parents well," Dorothy says. "Known them all since they were infants. What beautiful children they've raised."

She closes the door behind us, nudging another cat, this one tabby and skittish, with her foot before it can escape into the hall. Then she leads us into the kitchen, where she swats away a third cat (calico and missing a bit of its left ear) who is about to nibble at a plate of cookies.

"None of that, Jemima. Those are for our guests." She fans her hand at the plate. "Please help yourselves. Snickerdoodles, fresh from the oven."

I think twice before taking a cookie from a plate Jemima probably already licked, but Azura reaches for one immediately. She takes a bite. "Delicious. Just like Dad's!"

Dorothy settles into a kitchen chair, stroking the white cat. "That's because *I* was the one who gave your father his first snickerdoodle recipe."

"Really?" Azura takes the seat across from her. She pulls out her camera and a small tripod, positioning them in front of Dorothy. "I thought he learned from my grandma."

Dorothy leans in. "Who do you think taught *her*? I've been sharing my cookie recipes with Creeksiders all my life. Your father, though, he really perfected the process. I couldn't be prouder."

"I had no idea!" Azura pops the rest of the cookie into her mouth and then finishes locking the tripod in place.

"We'll have to get that on camera," I say, a little more intrigued than before. After so many of these interviews, I've come to expect unexpected Creeksider connections. It's a small world, and small-town living makes it even smaller. "Do we have your consent to record you?"

"Of course, love," says Dorothy. "Though I don't think I have much to say." The chubby fluff ball in her arms purrs as if in agreement.

I pull out my notebook with my list of interview questions. "I'm sure you do. Let's see . . . What's one of your favorite things about Creekside?"

"Maybe it's cliché, but I love our tree," she laughs. "That oak's the longest living citizen of this town. I remember climbing it as a girl. Used to sit in this U-shaped crook high up top for hours with my sketchpad. I'd draw birds and squirrels. Sometimes the creepy-crawlies burrowing between the bark. Lots of memories in that wood. Sad to see it getting sick like it is."

"Makes me sad too." I think about the story my parents tell every year on my birthday. How they couldn't have kids. How they wished on the tree for a child. The tree means so much to all of us—I can't imagine Creekside without it. I get a funny feeling in my stomach just thinking about it. "Seems like everyone's connected to it in some way," I say. I want to ask her another question about the tree, but Azura will get on me if I don't stick to our list, so I ask the next question. "And what's your oldest memory of living in Creekside, Mrs. Van Otten?"

Her eyes glaze over. "I suppose it goes back to baking with my mother. Chocolate chip cookies were her specialty. Crispy edges and gooey centers. She always let me lick the spoon after we mixed the batter." She sets the white cat on the floor and scoots her chair back. "As a matter of fact . . ."

She moseys to the counter near the sink and lifts something from the drying rack. She returns, brandishing it like a sword. "This is that very wooden spoon. Same spoon I used to mix these snickerdoodles. Mama used to say it was the secret ingredient in her baking. Nothing she ever made with it turned out wrong."

"Can I see it?" Azura asks.

Dorothy hands it to her. She inspects the spoon. "Looks pretty old."

She hands the spoon to me.

The instant it falls into my hand, a bizarre feeling comes over me. It's like I've known this spoon all my life. Like déjà vu but with touch. But I *know* I've never held this spoon before. I've never been inside Dorothy's apartment, let alone talked with her before today. Yet the feel of the handle is so natural in my palm, it's like it's always belonged there. It's almost warm too, like it's been sitting on a hot stove.

"Where did you get this?" I ask.

"Been in the family for ages," Dorothy says. "My father carved it from a fallen branch off the old oak out in Creekside Park."

The interview goes on, but my mind is stuck on the tree. Everyone in Creekside seems to care about it, but no one knows how to keep it from dying. I wish I could. The tree is a part of my story. Losing it would be like losing a part of me.

SUBJECT: DR. TABITHA WILSON

. . . .

MATTEO LORENZINI

What do you love most about Creekside?

DR. TABITHA WILSON

So many things, but my patients mostly. They feel more like family. It's nice, being able to care for my community in such a real way. It gives me purpose.

MATTEO LORENZINI

It's got to be hard sometimes, always seeing people you care about hurting.

DR. TABITHA WILSON

That's true. But seeing them heal makes it all worth it.

TEN

When I get home from our interview with Dorothy, Mom greets me with a pair of socks in her hands. And not just any socks. My baseball socks. The leafy ones that made a mess in my room. I've been so preoccupied with everything else that I totally forgot to clean up. Oops.

"I was going to run a load of laundry and I found these." She cocks her eyebrow and her hip. "There were crushed up leaves all over your room. On your blanket, on your floor. What have I told you about walking outside in your socks?"

I don't normally lie, but I legit have no idea how to explain the leaves, and I'm not getting into trouble for something I didn't do. I'm still caught up thinking about our interview with Dorothy too. I've felt off ever since I held that spoon, which is weird. It's a *spoon*. So whether I really mean to lie or not, what I say comes out less than honest. "I was working on a leaf project. For school. Got messier than I thought it would. Sorry."

A sudden itch spider-walks across my chest. I shift on my feet.

"A project?" Mom's lips wrinkle. "Why are you making that face? Is there something you're not telling me?"

Heat creeps up the back of my neck. I make myself look at her to prove I'm not lying. "What? No. I just didn't realize I'd made such a mess. I promise I'll clean it up."

As the words come out, my skin flares to mosquito-bite levels of irritation. I scratch near my heart, and my fingers catch on something coarse beneath my shirt. My stomach somersaults. Something doesn't feel right. My skin, it—

"Matteo, I—" She comes closer. "Are you okay?"

I sidestep around her and onto the staircase. "I'm totally fine, Mom. Stop worrying about everything." Then I turn and march upstairs, my hand clutching my chest.

She calls after me, "Your dad'll be home soon. He wants to warm up with you before you go to baseball practice tonight!"

I groan as I close my bedroom door. I totally want to and need to practice, but that's so not where my brain is at right now. My fingers run down the front of my shirt. It doesn't even feel like *skin* underneath the fabric. It's hard and rough. My hand falls to my side. Sweat sticks in my armpits. I force myself to the mirror above my dresser. I bite my lip. My chest is puffed out awkwardly. I fidget hesitantly with the bottom of my shirt. Then I slowly lift the fabric up.

The air in my lungs vanishes. I can't believe what I'm seeing. Stretched across my skin, from my left shoulder to just above my belly button, are dark brown calluses. "What the . . . ?" The growths protrude from my chest, ugly and swollen. I gingerly touch the one above my heart. It's solid, hard as stone.

I pick at a corner of crusty brown shell. A diamond-shaped fleck comes off. It doesn't hurt, and there's pink flesh underneath, not a bloody wound like I was afraid I'd find. That's a relief.

I roll the scabby thing between my fingers, holding it up in the afternoon light.

"It looks like . . ." But I can't bring myself to say it. It's too absurd.

Cricket loops around his bowl, completely unconcerned with the fact that my body is majorly malfunctioning. "Do you think I'm sick?" I say, trying to rationalize this. "Or maybe it's an allergy? Are these scabs or blisters? What does poison ivy look like?"

He circles round again. *"Don't ask me, I'm just a fish,"* I say in my Cricket voice. *"What you need is a doctor."*

I turn back to the mirror. "I bet Dr. Wilson's never seen anything like this."

Cricket dips down into a clump of plastic weeds.

"And now you're hiding from me?" I pick a fleck of brown off my chest. "I guess I'd hide from me too."

I pick and talk about what this could possibly be and pick some more until Dad calls me downstairs an hour later. Just great. It's time to warm up before baseball practice, and there's an anthill of brown scabs on my bed. But at least my skin is soft and normal-looking again.

Instead of brushing the stuff into the trash where Mom might find it, I open my window and toss it into the bushes, where I hope it'll blend in with the dirt and mulch.

Then, my hand on the doorknob, I take a deep breath. *Everything is fine*, I tell myself. *I'm totally fine. Nothing to worry about. Just smile at Mom and Dad. They don't need to know anything's wrong. All you need to worry about is baseball.*

My eyes wander to the Lorenzini bat, the wooden one Dad gave me for my birthday. It's leaning against my dresser. What I wouldn't give for some of that Lorenzini legacy to rub off on me. Slowly, I reach for the handle. My fingers wrap around the worn wood—and I snap back. It's *warm*. The same kind of warm I felt when I held Dorothy's spoon.

And that gets me thinking. Dorothy said her spoon was made from the tree in the park. Could the bat be too? Maybe I'm having some sort of allergic reaction to them. I need to be sure. In a last-second decision, I snatch the bat from the floor.

When I get downstairs, Dad's baseball glove is already on his left hand and there's a baseball in the other. "Ready?"

"Yeah, but . . . can I ask you a question first?" I hold the family bat out. "Where did this come from?"

"It was mine, and before that—well, you know the story," he says.

"But like . . . where did the wood come from?"

Dad pauses, rubbing his stubble with his right hand. "I think the story goes that one of my great-great-grandfathers carved it from a limb off the old oak in the park."

Holy. CRAP. I am buzzing on the inside. I was right. The tree *is* following me. But what does it mean? *Am* I allergic to it? And what does it have to do with *me*? What is it *doing* to me? The bat, the spoon, the growths on my skin . . .

Then it dawns on me.

The tree's *sick*. Could it be making *me* sick?

Dad tosses my glove, and I barely catch it I'm so lost in thought. "Come on," he says. "Let's get that bruised arm moving. Need you in primo shape before your second game."

I shake away my daze and turn on my Perfect Son face, even though I'm sure Dad can see right through it. "Right! Let's do this!"

But he swings his arm around me like nothing's wrong. "That's the spirit!"

Relieved, and maybe a little disappointed, I pull on the glove and follow him outside, ignoring the twisting in my gut and trying my best not to stare at the bushes beneath my bedroom window.

CREEKSIDE DOCUMENTARY TRANSCRIPT #10

SUBJECT: CHELSEA GERALDO

• •

CHELSEA GERALDO

My favorite thing in Creekside is actually your dad's bakery, Azura. His cupcakes are sinful.

AZURA GONZALEZ

You know he's single, right?

MATTEO LORENZINI

Azura.

CHELSEA GERALDO

Excuse me?

AZURA GONZALEZ

What? It's a fact. I'm just saying.

CHELSEA GERALDO

What's the purpose of this interview again?

ELEVEN

Saturday is April 1, April Fools' Day, and I'm pretty sure the joke's on me. I haven't had any other weird growths all week. I'm relieved, but I also feel like I'm totally losing my mind. I got so caught up worrying that the tree made me sick because I'd touched a spoon and a bat made from its wood, that I barely practiced. Now I'm sitting on the bench, drenched in mist, nervous I'm going to bomb worse than our first game. To top it all off, the sky is foggy gray and it's *cold*. Soggy cotton-ball clouds puff one after the other for miles in all directions.

I get called to bat at the bottom of the fourth inning. Coach Mathis claps me on the back and mumbles something about getting out of the ball's way—or maybe he says something about getting out of *my* own way? I'm not sure. It doesn't matter. *Just focus on hitting the ball*, I tell myself.

Today we're playing the Silver Cats. Their pitcher is a

tall boy with dark brown skin. He's struck out the last two Blue Whales, Omar included. This kid means business. How I can possibly get a hit with him pitching is beyond me.

Dad and Mom kept saying they believe in me all morning, which really means they *expect* me to do this. I've gotta try, for Dad especially. I grip the bat and mutter out loud, "I can do this."

Mist catches on my eyelashes. The Silver Cat hurls the first pitch. I swing and miss. The crowd sighs. I sigh even louder, but at least I actually *swung* this time.

"C'mon, Matteo. Keep your eye on the ball!" Dad hollers behind me.

A flicker of frustration tenses my muscles. Where does he *think* I'm looking? Of course my eyes are on the ball. That doesn't make it easier to hit!

A less-friendly voice calls behind me, "Don't miss, wuss."

My head whips back. Tyler, who's on deck, swings his bat like a golf club. He waggles his eyebrows at me. I scowl; I'm cold, I'm confused, and now I'm getting ticked.

Tyler hasn't called me by my name all week. *Matty* turned into *wuss* sometime on Thursday. I hate that word. Coach stands just a little way off in his translucent blue poncho. Even though I'm pretty sure he heard Tyler, he doesn't call him out, which makes me even angrier.

Fine. I choke up on the bat, my hands sliding higher on

the handle. *I'll show him who the wuss is.*

The ball comes at me. I throw my whole weight into the swing.

"Strike two," the umpire calls.

UGH. What is wrong with me? It's not *that* hard to hit a baseball. Lots of kids do it. I can do it at home and at practice (sometimes). Maybe Tyler's right. Maybe I *am* a wuss. Why can't I just freaking do this?

On the mound, the pitcher spins the baseball in his glove. His shoulder hitches. Then he lobs the ball. My eyes never leave the speeding white orb.

I can do this.

I swing.

The umpire hikes his thumb over his shoulder. "Strike three! You're out."

I'm so frustrated, so freaking angry, that I slam my bat on the ground.

"None of that," the umpire chastises me. "Back to the bench."

The tone of his voice stops me short. *I* don't get yelled at. I'm a *good* kid. I start to apologize, but the umpire's already moved on, his attention on Tyler, who slides past me, a glob of saliva prepped in his cheek for his ceremonial loogie.

Coach Mathis is at my side. "You okay, Lorenzini?"

"I'm fine," I lie. A tickle radiates across my skin all the way down to my ankles.

I try to breeze past him, but there's a sickening *crrrr-UNCH* when I bend my knee. I freeze midstep. I look down.

No, no, no. Not again. It's been days! Why NOW?

Freddie grimaces. "Ew. Was that your bones?"

"What? No!" My hands fly to my knees. Under my base-ball pants, I can feel coarse, scabby growths. I look down. My eyes widen. A corner of hard brown callus has torn through the white fabric.

"Did you hear his knees?" Freddie chuckles to Omar. "He's got total geezer bones."

I'm freezing, soaked, and my body is freaking out. And where does Freddie get off making fun of me? *He* always smells like raw onions! Red-hot fury rages inside my chest. I want to tell him off, but the words don't come. They're stuck somewhere in my rib cage, burning me from the inside out.

"Are you okay?" Omar asks, shoving past Freddie.

"I don't want to talk about it."

He glances down at my knees. "Your legs, they—"

"Just leave me alone." I feel a little bad for snapping at him, since it seems like he's trying to be nice. But all I want is to get away and figure out what the heck is happening to me.

CREEKSIDE DOCUMENTARY TRANSCRIPT #11

SUBJECT: CASIMIR KOWALSKI

. . . .

MATTEO LORENZINI

You've lived in Creekside a long time. I was wondering if you could tell us about the tree in Creekside Park?

CASIMIR KOWALSKI

I don't have anything to say about that tree.

MATTEO LORENZINI

Sure you do. Everyone in town does.

CASIMIR KOWALSKI

I'd rather talk about something else.

MATTEO LORENZINI

But—

CASIMIR KOWALSKI

No buts, Mr. Lorenzini.

TWELVE

I walk home with my baseball gear bag in front of my legs. Mom and Dad keep talking about "perseverance" and "next time." I nod along like I'm listening, but I'm totally distracted, worried they'll notice my legs. I replay the online search results I did earlier this week, trying to figure out what the actual what is going on with me. When we get back, I tell them I'm tired. That I want to be left alone. Fortunately, they let me be.

When I get up to my room, I drop my bag and strip off my damp baseball pants, anxious about what's hiding underneath. A slow hiss passes between my lips as I pull the fabric down.

From my thigh to my ankle, crusty brown calluses pucker over my skin. It's the same thing that happened to my chest. My fingers travel the rough surface. The growth is broken at my knee from me bending my leg. Sharp brown edges bite into the backside of my leg.

I examine the whorls. The eddies and curves, the edges and valleys. If it weren't so terrifying, it might be cool. Magical even. And there's no lying to myself anymore about what this is, even though I don't want it to be true. Even though it *can't* be true. I thought it might be poison ivy or poison oak, but this doesn't look anything like what came up when I googled "tree skin sickness" and "oak allergies." Then I thought it might be warts or boils or something even grosser, but it doesn't look anything like those pictures either!

There's only one thing it can be, unbelievable as it is. Tree bark. There's no mistaking it. I've looked at hundreds of images now. My legs are twin freaking saplings.

I pick at the bark on my legs. The crust peels off easily. While I free myself from the layer of wood, I confide in the only living thing who knows my secret. "Cricket, I don't get it. How am I growing bark?" Maybe the oak in the park could have made me sick, but I haven't been anywhere near it in weeks. Even then, I don't remember *touching* it. But maybe it's been sick longer than anyone realized. Maybe it really was the bat that did this to me. "But that doesn't make sense. It's impossible!"

Cricket stares at his reflection in the glass. *"So is growing bark,"* I say in my Cricket voice.

"Do *you* really think the tree did this to me?" I say.

Cricket swims away. I stop picking to dot the top of his fishbowl with food. A crust of my dark brown wood accidently tumbles in with it. Gross. I fish it out, afraid he might eat it. With food floating overhead, Cricket is suddenly much more interested in what I've got to say. He bobs up, his lips flashing open. I wish he could talk. He's a good listener, but that's not enough anymore. Of course, there's Mom and Dad, but they'll lose their minds if they think I'm sick. "I can't tell them, but I've got to tell someone."

He gobbles an orange flake. *"I'm someone."*

"I mean someone other than *you*."

My goldfish blows a bubble. I go back to picking at my legs.

"I suppose you could tell a human friend." Another piece of bark snaps off in my palm.

"Yeah, that's what I'll do," I say. "I'll tell Azura. She's smart. And she's heard all sorts of weird stories about the tree too, thanks to the documentary. Maybe she'll have an idea about what this is or how to help."

The fish food is nearly gone from the water's surface, but Cricket keeps gulping air, like a baby bird waiting for more food to drop down.

Or, almost, like he really has something to say.

CREEKSIDE DOCUMENTARY TRANSCRIPT #12

SUBJECT: SERGIO GONZALEZ

. . . .

SERGIO GONZALEZ

My pops started this bakery after he married my mom, so I grew up smelling like a loaf of bread.

MATTEO LORENZINI

Fascinating. And, Mr. Gonzalez, are you aware that your daughter is trying to set you up with our guidance counselor, Ms. Geraldo?

AZURA GONZALEZ

Matteo!

SERGIO GONZALEZ

I was not.

AZURA GONZALEZ

She's really nice!

SERGIO GONZALEZ

Really?

AZURA GONZALEZ

Really.

SERGIO GONZALEZ

Take her these cookies.

THIRTEEN

I've got a new theory about what triggers the tree-growing freak-outs—it hit me when I lied to Azura earlier today about not feeling well and a leaf popped out of my thumb. I shoved my hand in my pocket right away, and she was so glued to another one of Omar's brother's viral videos that I don't think she noticed. But this whole bark-growing THING is so ridiculous that I can't bring myself to say anything until we're walking home from school.

"I need to tell you something. In private." My head spins nervously up and down the sidewalk. We're alone, but you can never be too careful in a small town. "Can we go to your dad's bakery?"

She was scrolling through our documentary interview clips on her phone, but now she slides it into her pocket. "A private conversation? I'm all ears."

Creekside Bakery is nestled between the movie theater and our dentist's office. It's warm and smells like yeast and sugar and heat. Mr. Gonzalez, Azura's dad, waves from behind the counter as we walk in. He's a big man with hairy arms. His skin is darker, ruddier than Azura's. He's in a black apron covered in flour poofs. "Hey! How's it going?" he asks. "School okay?"

"It was whatever," says Azura. "We're just gonna hang out for a little bit."

"Hi, Mr. Gonzalez." I wave.

"You need anything?" he asks.

"We're good," says Azura. "Thanks though."

"I'll bring out a treat anyway." He winks at us and then disappears behind a curtain.

We sit at a small table next to the window, looking out over downtown Creekside. A young Asian woman in a green blazer walks by with a small girl's hand in her own. Azura leans over the table. "So, what's up, buttercup?"

My gaze drifts back to her. My toes curl in my shoes. *You can do this*, I think.

But now that it's time to put the words out there, I'm a tumbleweed of nerves. Maybe I shouldn't say anything. Maybe I should keep hiding and figure this out on my own. Maybe saying it out loud is going to make it worse.

Azura must see how anxious I am because she says, "Matteo, you can tell me anything." She leans in. "Is this about Omar?"

I jolt back. "What? No."

She raises an eyebrow. "Really?"

"No, it's . . ." I breathe in. "Something strange has been going on with me."

"Like what?"

"I don't know. There's been these weird . . . reactions I've been having."

"Like allergies?"

"Not exactly."

Mr. Gonzalez bustles through the curtain with a pair of muffins. The golden-domed cakes perfume the air. "Blueberry," he chimes. "Fresh this morning." He sets a plate in front of each of us. "I'm finishing up some business in back. Almost done with the design for the bicentennial celebration cookies! Holler if you need me, okay?"

"Thanks, Dad," says Azura.

"Thank you, Mr. Gonzalez," I add.

"Anything for you punks." Then he's gone and it's just the two of us again.

"You were saying?" Azura bites into her muffin. Purple-blue berry stains her front teeth.

I'm so nervous I can't even think about eating. The moment's here. I'm going to say it. I'm just going to say it. "I think I'm turning into a tree."

Azura covers her mouth too late. She laughs and spits muffin crumbs all over the place. "Riiiiiight. Good one, Matteo."

My ankles cross under the table. "I'm not kidding."

She stares at me like she's waiting for a "gotcha!" The air around us turns stale. I sit on my hands. The silence drags on. I start to sweat. Oh God. I made a HUGE mistake.

"Wait . . ." she says. "You're serious?"

I nod. My insides are screaming. This is the absolute WORST. She totally thinks I'm a freak. But, like, what was I expecting her to say? *Oh, that's cool? Me too?* Come on, Matteo!

She rubs her temples. "Okay. Um. Turning into a tree. What does that even mean?"

Deep breaths. Okay. This is better. She's listening. She's not freaking out.

Slowly, I say, "It first started when I lied to my mom when she found leaves in my—" I stop. I can't believe I didn't realize it before. "There were *leaves in my socks*. After the first baseball game. I thought I put on dirty socks, but that must have been me too!" I go on telling her about the bark covering my chest and how my legs turned into mini-trunks at the last game. With each new twist in the story, Azura's eyes widen a little more, but she doesn't jump in or tell me to stop. She doesn't even look disgusted. She just listens. And when I'm done, I feel lighter. I hadn't realized how heavy it was, carrying that secret around. For the first time in more than a week, I almost smile.

"Can you show me?" she says.

"What?"

"Do something tree-ish. I want to see!"

"It doesn't work that way." I shift in my chair. "I can't just make it happen. I—I don't know how." But that's not entirely true. And as proof, a leaf unfurls from the tip of my nose. "Okay. I lied. Which seems to make it happen. I grew bark when I lied to Coach and then later to my mom. I even sprouted a leaf today when I lied to you about being okay. That's when it hit me that I only grow when I don't tell the truth!" I pinch the leaf from my nose and offer it to her. "It's weird, right?"

She takes it gingerly, her eyes round as silver dollars. "Matteo, this is incredible."

"You don't think I'm a freak?"

"Are you kidding me?" she says. "It's the *freaking* coolest thing I've ever seen!"

"But why is this happening? What's wrong with me?"

She spins the stem between her fingers. "What you should be asking is, What's *right* with me? I'm glad you came to me. We'll get to the bottom of this." She grins, her hands flashing in the air. "I can see it now: Matteo, the Amazing Growing Boy!"

"Suuuuuure," I laugh. Leave it to her to spin what's happening into something good. "But I'm serious. I can't control this. Even if I never tell another lie in my life, I don't know if that's the only rule. What if I go full bark and leaves? What if I can't get it to come off?" My gaze sinks to the table, voice quieting. "I don't know what I'll do if my parents find out."

The leaf stops spinning in her hand. "Wait. You haven't told your *parents* yet?"

"No way! They want me to be this perfect boy, but I'm not. How do you think they'll react when they find out their miracle kid needs to be repotted instead of getting braces?"

"I'm sure they'll find you a very nice pot," Azura giggles. When I frown, she quickly adds, "You won't know if you don't give them the chance."

"You know my parents. As soon as they think something's wrong with me, they take over. Dad especially. The best thing I can do is figure out what's happening and how to fix it myself before they get a chance to lose their minds."

Azura licks the crumbs from her finger. "What if you can't fix it?"

"Don't even say that!"

"Would it be so bad? Does it hurt when the tree stuff happens?"

I shake my head. "Not really. But it's embarrassing."

She tucks her hair behind her ears. Now she means business. "Maybe you're one of those tree creatures from Lord of the Rings! What're they called? Oh, an ent!"

"I'm not an ent."

She smirks. "Okay, but that *would* be kind of cool."

"You're not helping."

"I'm *totally* helping."

"I shouldn't have told you."

"Of course you should have," she says. "Seriously. Why does this have to be a bad thing? Matteo, it's okay to *like* who you are."

"But *this* isn't who I am!" I snatch the leaf from her and crush it in my hand. "And if it is, I don't want it to be."

"Look at me." She waits to go on until I do. Her face is kind but stern. "I'm not gonna listen to you talk bad about yourself. But I will help you find answers. If that's what you want. But no more cutting yourself down." She chuckles. "See what I did there? Cut down? Tree?"

I struggle not to smile as I consider her offer. She doesn't need to know *everything* going on in my brain. I can think whatever I want about myself.

"Fine," I say, holding out my hand to shake. "You've got a deal."

CREEKSIDE DOCUMENTARY TRANSCRIPT #13

SUBJECT: MAYOR MEYERS

. . . .

MAYOR MEYERS

People kept carving hearts in the tree. Initials too. You've seen them, I'm sure. Started sweet, but the more folks did it, the more the tree looked vandalized. We put a stop to that a few years back.

MATTEO LORENZINI

Why do you think so many Creeksiders want to make their mark on the tree?

MAYOR MEYERS

Oh, it goes back to those silly folktales. Some say that if you carve your initials in the oak, you'll be bound to each other forever. Others say the tree will bring you good luck. All nonsense, of course.

FOURTEEN

After I spill everything I've been worrying about to Azura, she's determined to solve my tree-growing problem like I'm the world's greatest puzzle. She's almost giddy. It's weird.

"So if the tree is making you sick, or if even half the stories in town about the tree are true, even if Mayor Meyers says the superstitions aren't real . . . well, what if the tree *is* magic? You said your parents tell you the same story every year on your birthday. I mean, there's gotta be something there, right?" Azura goes on and on the whole way to Creekside Park. We—*she*—decided the only way to get to the bottom of all this is to visit the tree. I've been to the tree a million times, but this is different. It might change everything I thought I knew about myself. I'm a little excited and little scared. Azura tucks a wisp of hair behind her ear. "Like your mom and dad pretty much begged the tree to give them a son and then you appeared! And then there's the bat and Dorothy's spoon. It's gotta be connected."

My shoes scuff the sidewalk. "I know, but I just can't believe wishing on a tree has anything to do with what's happening to me. It's a story. It's *like* magic. Not *actual* magic."

"We'll see about that," she says, plodding through the Creekside Park archway.

It's nearly twilight, and the park is almost completely empty except for us. We climb up the little hill to the ancient oak. A cool breeze slips through the branches. My skin prickles. The lower boughs spread like octopus arms. Most of the branches are just beginning to bud, so the naked limbs look like the lobes of a brain. The grass underneath the tree was recently seeded; yellow-green pellets dot the ground. A pair of squirrels chase each other up the trunk.

Azura stares at me, hands on her hips. "So?"

"So what?"

"Do you feel anything?" she asks, eyeing my arms, my legs, my hair.

I scour my skin. "Not really. I've got some goose bumps, but it's kind of chilly, so . . ." I look around and then whisper, "No tree things."

She looks unconvinced. "We should look around. Maybe we'll find something."

"But what are we looking *for*?"

"*You're* the one sprouting," she says. "Maybe you'll know it when you . . . *grow* it?" She giggles.

"That doesn't even make sense." I laugh.

"It doesn't have to make sense for it to be true!" she says in a singsong voice, moseying to the left of the tree. Her eyes rove up the trunk.

I wander in the opposite direction and inhale the earthy smell. Wet dirt and bark. Buds like gems glisten on finger-bone branches. I stop when I see the dark, jagged scar zigzagging up the trunk. Dark brown sap leaks from the edges of the wound. It looks way worse than I remember, or maybe I'm just really taking a good look at it now. I shuffle back a step. Is that what's going to happen to me next? Will I break open and leak sludge?

I keep walking and nearly trip over a mason jar cozied between two roots. Inside is an unlit candle, slightly melted and drooping to one side. The jar is gray and cloudy from smoke.

In the wood above the jar are old carvings of initials. Creeksiders aren't allowed to cut into the tree, but that hasn't stopped many people. Traditions are stronger than rules sometimes. My eyes drift to a heart underneath a sagging limb. Inside are two sets of initials I know well.

"We came here on our first date," I remember Mom saying when I was younger. She and Dad brought me to the oak for a picnic on their anniversary when I was four or five. "Your dad packed us a basket of food and drinks. It was very romantic. Then he carved our initials, see?" Then she whispered in my ear, "But you can't tell anyone, or you'll get us into trouble." She tickled me, and I burst into a fit of laughter.

I stretch my hand up, feeling the grooves in the wood where *VL + DD* are etched. My parents are part of this tree. Maybe that means something. Then my eyes wander to all the other hearts and initials, some newer cut, some well-worn. There are so many. Why would my parents be special? It doesn't make sense. Then my eye catches one carving almost faded back into the bark. The message is different from the rest. Instead of a pair of initials, it says *For LL.*

My fingers are drawn to the initials. They press into the letters. The tree is warm despite the chill. A strange feeling comes over me, strong and sudden. *Uh-oh.* It builds up from my toes and fizzes out my fingers. I pull my hand back, but it's too late. Bright green buds, no larger than heads of baby's breath, break through the bark where my fingers just were, covering the *For LL* carving. I gasp. Each bud unfurls into a shiny little leaf. A shape takes form in the green. Three letters—no. A word?

KAZ.

"Whoa."

I turn around, not realizing Azura was standing behind me, watching the whole thing.

"What does it mean?" I ask.

"That you are officially the coolest person I know."

"No," I say, pointing to the leaves. "That! What's a 'kaz'?"

Azura cocks her head and bites her lip. She does this sometimes when she's thinking. "I'm not sure." Then she grins. "But we know one thing for sure now. The tree *is* the answer."

Before I can respond, a gruff voice calls behind us, "What do you think you're doing?"

CREEKSIDE DOCUMENTARY TRANSCRIPT #14

SUBJECT: FREDDIE MCCOY

. . . .

FREDDIE MCCOY

I lost a kite in the tree once. Got stuck way up. Too high to climb and get down. But the weirdest thing happened.

MATTEO LORENZINI

What?

FREDDIE MCCOY

This is gonna sound creepy, but, like, the next day, it was on my front porch.

AZURA GONZALEZ

Someone got it down for you?

FREDDIE MCCOY

No clue. It was just there, like it flew back all on its own.

FIFTEEN

Officer Ian James marches toward us, the bright beam of a flashlight pointed in our faces. We shield our eyes. I scowl. It's not even that dark yet. What the heck?

"Don't you know the park closes at dark?" he says. Officer James is a burly white man with rosy skin and a thin goatee. His blue uniform is crisp and pressed. His silver belt buckle glistens.

I glance to my left. A pale streak of sunset wanes on the horizon. "It's still twilight."

Azura elbows me. "Don't talk back to an *officer.*"

I hadn't meant to talk back. I was just stating facts, but she's right. "Sorry."

Officer James clicks his flashlight off, stashes it in a holster at his hip, and hooks his thumbs in his pockets. "What're you two doing out here so late?"

"Research," Azura and I say at the same time. I love when our brain waves sync.

His right eyebrow arches. "Oh yeah? What for?"

"School project," says Azura.

"Getting ready for Arbor Day," I add. Azura looks at me like she's impressed by the lie. But my scalp tingles and a leaf sprouts behind my ear. *Oh crap.* I was so caught off guard by Officer James that I forgot I have to tell the truth or my secret will get out! I scratch the leaf away as nonchalantly as I can. Officer James doesn't seem to notice—thank God.

"I see," he says, drawing out the *e* nice and long. "Still, can't have minors wandering out here after sundown." His eyes climb the branches, which, in the fading light, look more and more like skeletal hands. "Sad. Thing's got a nasty blight."

Azura and I exchange a glance. "What is a blight exactly?" she asks.

I curl my fingers into my palm. I'm not sure I want to know.

Officer James nods toward the park exit. "C'mon. I'll tell you while I walk you home."

We follow him, his flashlight clicking on again, this time with the beam facing away from us on the uneven ground. "That dark streak along the trunk?" he says. "Sometimes trees get fungal infections or infested with insects. When that happens, they start dying from the inside out. Sap turns the wrong shade. Bark falls off. It can spread and start killing off nearby plants. That's why it's coming down after the bicentennial celebration in a few weeks."

I stop in my tracks. "They're cutting it down? But we were just talking to Mayor Meyers about the tree. She didn't say anything about that!"

Officer James shrugs. "Authorization for the tree's removal only got approved a few days ago. But yep—Creekside and that oak'll be saying goodbye in couple weeks."

Azura glances uneasily at me and then back at the tree. "But the branches look healthy. How do you know the insides are messed up?"

"If the sickness is coming through the bark like it is, that's bad news bears," says Officer James. I cringe. "That tree's been dying near on a decade now, though it seems to have gotten much worse in the past few weeks. Can't say I'll be sad to see it go."

We pass under the park archway and onto Main Street. I ask, "Why not?"

"You know how many 9-1-1 calls I get because of that tree? Kids who think they can climb it and get stuck or fall out and break an arm, an elbow, a whatever. Cats chasing birds, stranding themselves high up." He coughs into his fist. "Branch came down a couple years back that nearly brained a guy to death. Thing's too old, too unstable. A tree shouldn't be trouble. If it's failing to be useful, I say we're better off without it."

Azura stops walking. "But the tree's Creekside's heart and soul. Even Mayor Meyers says so. A town can't survive without those."

"We very well might have to." Officer James chuckles.

I shudder.

"Can't they make it better?" Azura asks. "There's got to be a tree doctor or something."

"Well, I'm no arborist, but I think it's too far gone for saving." Officer James points down the sidewalk. "You two head on home now, and don't worry anymore about that tree. Have a good night." Then he walks off in the opposite direction, whistling to himself, his flashlight beam bobbing on the sidewalk.

Azura's worried eyes turn to me. "What now?"

I gulp. "I don't know."

CREEKSIDE DOCUMENTARY TRANSCRIPT #15

SUBJECT: DOROTHY VAN OTTEN

. . . .

DOROTHY VAN OTTEN

Oh, I've heard some say that oak was blessed by angels. Vanessa, in apartment three, she told me that when she was little, she swore she saw angels hovering above the branches one Christmas Eve.

MATTEO LORENZINI

Do you think she was telling the truth? Did you ever see that?

DOROTHY VAN OTTEN

She's a little dramatic but not one to fib. And nope, never saw anything like that myself. Still, I believe anything's possible.

SIXTEEN

After I wave goodbye to Azura, I walk inside my house, my mind swirling. How can a tree grow leaves in the shape of words? Did I hallucinate that? No, Azura saw it too. But maybe we were both hallucinating. Is that possible? And what even is a kaz? Or is it *who is* Kaz? Maybe KAZ stands for something. Kids Acting Zippy. Kings Above Zeroes. Keep Asking—man, Z's a tough one. Zombies? Kill All Zombies? I laugh. No, that can't be it.

Then again, what if it *is* about death? That sap oozing from the gash was pretty gross. I can only imagine the nastiness hidden inside the trunk. Then a darker thought hits me. What if *I'm* just as nasty on the inside? Please no.

I swing open my bedroom door, saying, "Cricket, you'll never guess what happened today. I was at the park with Azura, and we—" I stop. Usually, Cricket's looping around or darting behind plants, but he's not moving. I step closer. "Cricket?"

I gasp. He's statue-still and belly up, floating on the surface like a discarded orange rind.

"No, no, no, no, no." I poke his scaley white stomach with my finger. "Come on. Wake up. Don't be dead. Don't be dead!"

But he is. He's gone. Gone *forever*. The one friend I could say *anything* to. My everything goes into nuclear meltdown. Cricket, the tree, my body—it's all too much. I can't do all this on my own. My shoulders shudder, and I run to Mom. I don't cry, because that would really make me a baby, but I wrap my arms around her without saying anything.

"Sweetie, what's the matter?" Her fingers run through my hair.

"It's Cricket," I mumble into her shirt. "He's dead."

She coos, "Oh no. I'm so sorry, Matteo. I guess it was his time to go to fishy heaven."

"Bill, hold on," Dad says, walking in from the other room with his cell phone pressed to his ear. I hide my face. I really didn't want him to see me like this. "What's wrong?" he asks.

"His fish," Mom says for me. "He died."

Dad's concerned expression melts into sympathy. He holds up a finger and says into his phone. "Bill, I'm gonna have to call you back." Then he hangs up and pats my head. "Sorry, bud. We'll take care of it. Okay?"

I let go of Mom. My words come out more jagged than I mean them to. "How? He's *dead*. It's not like you can bring him back."

Dad frowns, but he doesn't chastise me for talking back. Instead, he and Mom take me into the living room. "Have a seat," she says. She gathers me under her arm. She smells like rose petals. "Take a breath."

"You're right," Dad says. "We can't bring him back, but we *can* get you a new fish."

"That's not what I want," I say. "I don't understand. He was fine this morning."

"Oh, honey," Mom says, stroking my cheek with the back of her hand. "These things happen. He's in a better place now. It's not your fault."

I frown. I hadn't thought it was my fault, but . . . what if it is? In the dirty dishwater of my mind, I pick out little things: maybe I forgot to feed him . . . no, I remember feeding him . . . but my bark did fall in his water the other day . . . OH NO. My *infected bark skin* was in his bowl! I sit up. All my blood drains to my toes. It *is* my fault. It's gotta be. If the tree got me sick, then *I* could have gotten Cricket sick. I scoot farther away from Mom. What if I get my parents sick too? What if we're all going to die because of me?

"Chin up, bud. Don't cry," Dad says. "We'll get you a new fish. Tomorrow. Promise."

Dang it! I pull the collar of my T-shirt over my cheeks. I hadn't even realized I'd started crying. "I—I don't want a new fish."

"You will tomorrow. You'll see." Dad steps closer. "We should probably flush him before he starts to stink up your room though."

My jaw drops. "You can't *flush* him." He's clearly lost his mind. You don't flush a friend. Not down the toilet like some . . . some . . . turd!

"Kiddo, that's what happens with fish." He scratches the side of his nose.

I leap up. "Absolutely not. I'm burying him. He deserves it."

"But he'll just get—"

Mom cuts Dad off. "If that's what you want, then that's what we'll do. We can bury him. But not tonight. Tomorrow, when you've had time to settle down."

I nod. The idea of not having to let him go right away makes me a feel little less awful. "Okay. Yeah. I like that better." I sniff. "I'm gonna say goodbye to him now."

"Sure, sport," Dad says. "Whatever you want."

I shove myself from the couch and trudge up the steps to my room.

"Hey there," I say like I normally would.

Cricket floats.

"I'm sorry you died." I stare at his silvery scales. "I—" I take a deep breath. "I really hope it's not my fault. And if it

102

is, I'm really, *really* sorry, Cricket." My finger rings the rim of the bowl. "I didn't mean to."

There's a trio of bubbles near his tail. One of them pops.

"You were a good listener," I say. "Thanks for that."

Another bubble bursts.

SUBJECT: VINCENZO LORENZINI

. . . .

MATTEO LORENZINI

What do you like most about Creekside?

VINCENZO LORENZINI

That we're such a close-knit community. No matter what, we've got each other's backs.

MATTEO LORENZINI

What do you think makes us such a close community?

VINCENZO LORENZINI

Well, when adversity strikes, we band together. We work as a unit to fix things. Like after the church fire a couple years back, we all raised money for the reconstruction. Had the whole project done in less than a year. Couldn't have done that without the whole town coming together.

SEVENTEEN

"I'm sorry about your fish." Azura chomps into a carrot stick. The cafeteria around us buzzes with conversation. Today's hot lunch is pizza, and everything smells like parmesan and garlic, which would be great if I wasn't stuck eating a peanut butter and jelly sandwich.

"Thanks," I say. "I'm gonna bury him after school. Want to come with?"

"Where are you going?" Omar asks, dropping into the seat next to me. I'm surprised to see him, but this'll be his third time eating with us now. Maybe I should be less surprised? Then again, he ditched me for so long, I don't think I'll ever stop being surprised when he actually shows up.

I'm still super-awkward around him too. Like I can't stop fidgeting or staring at him for too long. I wonder if my breath smells as I say, "To bury my goldfish. He died. Last night. By accident. I didn't kill him."

Omar laughs. "I didn't think you did, but I'm sorry that happened. I had a hermit crab that died. That *was* my fault. Forgot to feed it."

"That's terrible," Azura gasps.

Omar's hands go up defensively. "I was only two years old! Blame my great-aunt for gifting a toddler a pet!"

"Still!" Azura turns to me. "I promised Dad I'd go straight home to work on my science project. I've been putting it off." Then she looks from me to Omar. A sly, subtle grin forms on her face. "But since you have experience with dead pets, Omar, maybe *you* could help Matteo?"

I kick her under the table. I know exactly what she's trying to do. Maybe he and I are friends (ish) again, but we only see each other at school or baseball. I haven't hung out with Omar, just the two of us, in a long time. I don't know if I even know how to anymore.

Before I can take back her invitation, he says, "Yeah, sure!"

The tips of my ears heat up. "You've probably got better things to do than a fish funeral."

He shrugs. "Not really."

"You *really* don't have to come."

He shrugs again. "I don't mind."

"Yeah, Matteo," says Azura. "Omar *wants* to come with you. It'll be fun."

"Leave it to you to put the 'fun' in funeral," I say dryly.

"More like *fin*, right?" says Omar.

Azura and I laugh. If he weren't so cute, I'd think that was the worst pun I've ever heard.

Then Tyler has to go and ruin the moment. "Omar! You're at the wrong table again!"

I shrink into my seat. I hate that he makes me feel so freaking small.

But Omar waves him off. "No, *you're* at the wrong table!"

Tyler mutters to Freddie, "Maybe Omar's got a crush. But is it on Azura . . . or Matteo?" Their table erupts in snickers. I turn a darker shade of red. Why did they have to make *that* joke? No way Omar's ever going to sit with us again now.

"They're such creeps," says Azura.

"Omar! Come on!" Freddie shouts.

Omar stands with a groan, and I crumple on the inside. "I'm just gonna go over there," he says. "They won't stop until I do." Then he looks at me. "But I'll see you after school, okay?"

"Yeah, okay." I want to believe he's not completely ditching me again for Tyler and Freddie, but I don't feel good about this. Chances are slim he'll actually show later. I watch silently as Omar picks up his tray and slumps to their table.

"Don't let them get to you," Azura says, chomping into another carrot. "Tyler's just jealous Omar wants to sit with you instead of him."

"Jealous?" I nibble my sandwich. Peanut butter sticks to the roof of my mouth. "No way he's jealous of *me*."

She leans over, her voice becoming a whisper. "I'm actually kind of glad he's gone. I wanted to talk to you about what happened yesterday in the park. I've been thinking."

"Yeah?" I say, running my tongue across my front teeth. "About the tree? That's all I've been able to think about. Other than Cricket." And now I'm worried those two things are connected and that I'm an accidental fish murderer!

"No. I mean, yes but *no*," says Azura. "I'm talking about *what happened* at the tree." Her voice gets quieter. "The leaf letters. K-A-Z?"

"Are you sure they were letters?" I ask. Part of me wants Azura to say this is all impossible. That it can't be real. That there's nothing wrong with me. "Maybe we were just seeing things. It was kinda dark."

"Not *that* dark," says Azura, clearly not reading my mind. "And they were definitely letters. At first, I thought they were initials. Like the ones you touched right before it happened?"

I nod. "It was more than initials. It said, '*For* LL.' Maybe K-A-Z and LL go together?"

"Oh, they've gotta be connected. You touched those words and BOOM," Azura says, "but I don't think K-A-Z are initials." She leans in. "What if it's a *word*?"

"I thought about that too." My brow scrunches. "But kaz? What kind of word is that?"

"Not a *word* word," Azura says smugly. "A *name*. A *nickname*."

"Wait. The tree has a name? Is that what it was trying to tell us?"

Azura massages her temples. "Matteo! No! I think the tree wants us to find a person, someone who might be able to help. Someone named Kaz."

I take another bite of my sandwich. "Well, I don't know anyone named Kaz."

Azura grins. "Yes, you do."

I set my sandwich down. "Who?"

"Our librarian," she says smugly. "Mr. Casimir 'Kaz' Kowalski."

CREEKSIDE DOCUMENTARY TRANSCRIPT #17

SUBJECT: VANESSA HOUGHTON

. . . .

VANESSA HOUGHTON

Dotty sent you, did she?

MATTEO LORENZINI

She says you saw something odd happen around the tree in Creekside Park. Something about angels?

VANESSA HOUGHTON

You got that right. It was near dead of winter. The whole tree was covered in ice. I swear the very Christmas star was shining above it, bright as the sun. The whole tree was glowing. Almost humming with light. The most beautiful thing I ever saw.

MATTEO LORENZINI

Did you ever see that happen again?

VANESSA HOUGHTON

Nope, but I know what I saw. And nobody's going to change my mind about that.

AZURA GONZALEZ

And nobody should.

EIGHTEEN

Azura and I stop by the library on the way to our next class, but the library assistant tells us Mr. Kowalski is on his lunch break.

"We'll talk to him tomorrow," Azura says. "First thing in the morning."

"You're sure he goes by Kaz?" I ask as we leave.

She sighs. "Okay, I don't *know* know, but Kaz *is* a nickname for Casimir. I googled it."

"And the internet is *always* right."

"No, but—just trust me on this, Matteo," she says. "Hurry up. We're gonna be late."

I don't argue with her, but the rest of the day, I can't make sense of how Mr. Kowalski could be connected to the old oak tree and whatever is going on with me. He's just an old man. No way he's got anything to do with magically growing, word-spelling leaves. And if we get him involved and he finds out what's happening to me, will he try to get

Mom and Dad involved? That absolutely cannot happen.

By the end of school, my brain is a lint trap of questions and all I can think about is the tree. How did it get sick? How could it make *me* sick? The more I think about it, the more I need answers. When the final bell rings, I bolt for the front entrance of the school. I scour the steps for Omar. There's Stevie and Daisy, Alicia and Freddie. But no Omar. I start to wilt. I'm such an idiot. Of course he's not here. Feeling like a total loser for believing he'd show up, I walk down the first step and a hand claps me on the back. I spin around, afraid it's Tyler with another dig about baseball.

But it's not him.

"Hey!" Omar says. "Sorry. My locker got stuck."

"You came." My lips smash shut. I didn't mean to say that out loud. But I'm so relieved to see him that it just came out!

He laughs awkwardly. "Uh, yeah."

I stand up taller, dropping my backpack casually down my shoulders as I try to look like I wasn't about to have a total freak-out. "Change of plans on the burial," I say. "Meet me at the park in fifteen minutes?"

When I get home, I toss my backpack on a chair in the living room, kiss Mom on the cheek, and bolt upstairs to get the shoebox with Cricket's corpse. Then I dash back down the stairs, box in hand, and make for the door, but Mom steps in front of me. "Where do you think you're off to?"

"I'm going to bury Cricket," I say. "In the park. I thought that might be nicer for him, instead of our backyard."

Her forehead creases. "The park? Is that allowed?"

I shrug. I hadn't thought about that. "I'll find out when I get there?"

She lifts her wrist to check her watch. "All right, fine. But make it quick. I want your homework done before dinner. Understand?"

"Yeah, I'll be fast," I say. I don't have time for this. Omar's going to be waiting for me. What if I'm late and he decides to leave?

Mom rubs my arm that got hit with the ball. The bruise is nearly gone now. "How are you feeling? With Cricket and everything? You were pretty upset last night. I've been worried about you all day."

"I'm fine," I say, which is only sort of true.

And just like that, a leaf pops out of my bellybutton. My hand slides over my stomach.

Mom gives me a suspicious look. "You sure?"

I nod, sweat beading on the back of my neck. "Yeah, I'm totally fine." Another leaf pops out against my hand. I spin to the door, hiding my stomach with Cricket's box. "I've got to go. I'm meeting Omar."

Her lips wrinkle into a side-of-her-mouth smirk. "Oh really? I thought you two weren't— Well, tell him I say hello," she says, and pulls me in for a hug, the shoebox (and my stomach leaves) squishing between us. "I love you."

"Love you too." I shimmy out of her embrace. "See you later!"

Mom's the best, but sometimes it's suffocating, her needing to know every little thing going on in my brain. I speed walk, hoping she didn't keep me from beating Omar to the park.

But just as I feared, he's already at the entrance. "Sorry I'm late," I say.

He shoves his cell phone in his pocket. "It's okay. I was watching a video my brother just posted. It's already got over four thousand views." He sighs. "Since he started high school, it's like the internet is the only way I get to see him."

"That kind of sucks," I say. I never knew his brother well, but his videos go viral all the time. Kids are always talking about them. "Sorry."

"Yeah, it's whatever." But his face tells me it's so not whatever. Before I can ask anything else about his brother, he nods his chin at my hands. "You put your fish in a shoebox?"

"Is that okay?" I ask, suddenly self-conscious about the decision.

He pokes the box, grinning. "I mean, sure. It's kind of like a mini-coffin."

I laugh. This is how he and I used to be. Maybe it won't be weird, just the two of us. Maybe we can still be friends.

Or friends *again*? I'd like that, but if I'm being *really* honest, someday I'd like to be *more* than friends. But I push those feelings down. I want a story like Mom and Dad's, which means I need to like girls. Not boys. Not Omar. I should like Azura. But I've tried and I don't. And that doesn't make me feel good at all.

Thoughts about boys and girls and stuff get swept away when we get to the tree. Goose bumps bubble up and down my arms. Even though I haven't lied, a tickle travels across my chest, and I try not to panic. I absolutely cannot get weird in front of Omar. No freaking way. He'll never want to be my friend again if I tree out, and I only just sort of got him back. He might stand up for me when it comes to baseball, but leaves and bark? There's got to be a line some-where.

But I majorly cannot keep my cool. My hands start to shake. The shoebox quivers in my grasp. What if something tree-ish happens, like those Kaz leaves that grew on the trunk? I can keep myself from lying, but what if there are other rules I don't know about yet? Clearly, I didn't think this through. *UGH, Matteo!* Bringing Omar here was a huge mistake.

"How about over here?" Omar asks, oblivious to my anxiety. He points to a divot between two elbows of root poking through the ground.

I kneel quickly, pressing my fingers into the soil. The earth is moist. "Yeah, let's just get this over with."

"How are we going to dig his grave?"

"Oh." I blush. "I didn't think about that."

"It's okay. We can use our hands." He shoves his sleeves up his forearms. He bends next to me, fingers clawing into the brown dirt. "I'll help."

We dig. Our hands rub against each other in the shallow hole. Each time it happens, a static shock attacks my heart. I try to focus on the dirt in my palms.

"Can I ask you something?" he says, suddenly serious.

I nod yes, even though I'm not sure I want him to ask whatever it is. If you have to ask about asking a question, that's not usually a good sign.

He sits back on his heels. "Did I do something wrong? You stopped hanging out with me last year, and I don't really understand what happened." He picks a piece of grass and twirls it between his fingers. "It sounds cheesy, but I, uh, I missed hanging out with you."

What the WHAT? That isn't at all what I expected him to say. "You—I—I thought *you* didn't want *me* around. After you made the Blue Whales and I didn't. You seemed pretty stoked about your new friends." Anger creeps into my voice. Where does *he* get off thinking *I'm* the problem? I'm talking too loudly, but I can't help it. "They didn't want anything to do with me, so I thought you didn't either." My eyes fall to the dirt. "At least, it sure seemed that way."

He flicks the blade of grass into the hole. "I didn't mean it to. You know the guys. They can be . . ."

"Jerks," I finish for him.

He nods. "*Huge* jerks." He sighs. "Honestly, I was intimidated by them at first. But then they started actually being kind of cool with me, and it wasn't so bad."

"So you stopped being my friend," I say. "That way they'd like you more?"

He can't seem to look at me now. "I guess that had something to do with it, but I honestly didn't think about it that way before. Now I feel like a total jerk." He reaches across the hole and grabs my shoulder. "I'm sorry. That was really crappy of me to ditch you. You were—you *are* one of my best friends. Can you forgive me?"

I really hope he can't feel my shoulder sweating. This is the moment I've wanted for months now. To have Omar back. For him to say these things. After getting hurt by him, I'm hesitant, but it seems like he really means his apology. And I so badly want to go back to how things were. How we used to laugh at corny jokes about farts and poop. How we could talk about nothing for hours and not get bored. I miss that. So much. So I say, "Yeah. We're good." I grin. "Let's get this finished."

He smirks. "*Fin*-ished." When I cringe, he adds, "Too soon, too soon."

But then I can't help but smile.

By the time we've dug a hole a foot wide and a foot deep, our hands are crusted with dirt and capped in crescents of black fingernail. I rest the shoebox in the hole, and a fog of sadness comes over me. This is it. The last time I'll be this close to Cricket. Silently, I say goodbye to my fish, willing myself not to get emotional. I don't want Omar thinking I'm a total baby. Still, Cricket was my friend, silly as that sounds. Turns out saying goodbye, even to a fish, isn't easy.

We cover the box with dirt. I pat the earth smooth.

Now that it's done, now that Cricket is really, truly gone, I can't help a rogue tear escaping. It drips from my eye to the soil, dotting the earth like a shadow.

Omar asks, "Hey, are you okay?"

"What? I'm fine." I sniff, rubbing my dirty hands on my pants.

Then a bright green stem sprouts where my tear fell. My eyes widen. I swipe the wet streak from my face. The twiggy stem shoots up an inch, then another, and another, until it's a foot tall. *Not good, not good, not good!* Leaves emerge from two arms of branch and the spearhead top. Just as suddenly as it began to grow, it stops. Inside, I'm a hot mess of panic. There's no way Omar didn't see my tear fall and magically grow into a baby tree. He's totally going to freak. I can't bring myself to look at him. A wind passes between us. The leaves on the little tree wave, as if in greeting.

I gulp.

Omar's the first to speak. "Ummm . . . did you see what I just saw?"

"I—" But I don't know what else to say. I didn't mean for that to happen. I don't even know *how* it happened. And Omar can't know I'm some tree-growing weirdo. "You didn't see anything," I say quickly. My skin starts to itch. "We should go."

"Hold up." He frowns. "I totally *did* see that. It was like . . . magic. We can't go *now*!"

"We absolutely can." I back away from the tree, but I stop when his eyes widen.

"Matteo . . ."

I follow his gaze to my hands.

Bright green leaves poke from my sleeves. My pulse speeds up. *No, no, no.* I shake my hands, hoping the leaves will fall to the ground and I can laugh it off like it's nothing. But the leaves don't drop—they *grow* farther out of my shirt. Up my arm, hidden from view, I feel more stemming from my skin. Sweat rises furiously on my forehead.

"Whoa," says Omar.

I tear at the leaves. They shred between my fingers by the handful. I try to find the right words to convince Omar that he's not seeing this, but my jaw's no longer connected to my teeth or lips or tongue. I sputter, "It's not—I'm not—"

More leaves spill out. That's my problem. There *aren't*

words for what's happening to me. Omar's a thousand percent gotta think I'm a freak. Worry funnel-clouds in my mind. He's totally gonna ditch me again and tell everyone I cry over dead fish and that I'm turning into a bizarro tree.

The urge to run comes over me again, but there's no bedroom or library to hide in. Just open space and this enormous oak looming over us. Now other people are starting to notice. A woman in a pink tracksuit jogs in place on the trail to our left, head cocked in our direction. A man sitting on a bench near a patch of tulips stares, adjusting the glasses on his nose. I tug my sleeves down, and Omar asks a terrible question. "Are you—are *you* doing that?"

He knows, he knows, he knows. There's no running from this. He's here. He sees me. So I say, "Yeah, I am." I wish the earth would swallow me whole.

But his eyebrows rise, and his lips spread into a giant grin. "That is so. Freaking. Cool."

CREEKSIDE DOCUMENTARY TRANSCRIPT #18

SUBJECT: DR. TABITHA WILSON

· ·

MATTEO LORENZINI

Have you heard any weird stories about the tree in Creekside Park?

TABITHA WILSON

Oh, sure. Everyone's got stories about that tree.

MATTEO LORENZINI

Tell us your favorite one.

TABITHA WILSON

Well, the most interesting story I ever heard was about how it got there in the first place. They say it was planted by a witch who cast a spell on it. Fed it magic so it could hear and see like people do, that it became her eyes and ears, and that's how she knew who was telling the truth when folks came to her for spells. They say she only helped people with good intentions. She was a healer. I like to think she and I have that in common.

AZURA GONZALEZ

So you think that story is true?

TABITHA WILSON

I think every story is true. Just a little.

NINETEEN

My insides flutter. Omar Jones thinks I'm *cool*. But I don't feel cool as more leaves come shooting out my sleeves.

"Dude," Omar says. "That's sick!"

A young couple holding hands let go of each other when they see me. The guy whispers something in the girl's ear. The jogger woman has come to a full stop now, and the man on the park bench is pulling out his phone. I yank the greenery from my sleeves, trying not to make too big a show of it. Emerald bunches pile on the ground. Then I take Omar by the arm. "Let's get out of here."

We dart down the hill and make for the exit.

"Can't you make it stop?" he asks.

"Don't you think I would if I could?" I say. I know I messed up lying to him about not seeing the little tree grow, but that was one little lie. Why am I still growing?

"Oh. Right."

"We can't go to my house," I say, turning out of the park. "Dad's at the firehouse, but Mom can't see me like this."

Omar's nose wrinkles. "Can't your mom help—"

"She doesn't know," I cut him off. "Neither of my parents do. And they *can't* know."

"What? Are you serious?" he says as we turn the corner onto my street, almost running into a woman and her toy poodle. "They don't know you have *superpowers?*"

The woman looks at me suspiciously over her sunglasses.

"Can you *not* right now?" I whisper, pulling him along and shooting my eyes in her direction.

Omar looks sheepish. "Oops. Sorry."

"I have an idea," I say, letting him go. "Follow me."

I can't go home looking like this, but Azura's house will be safe. Mr. Gonzalez always works late at the bakery, so I won't have to hide it from him. The only tricky thing is getting inside Azura's house without Mom seeing. She has a habit of peeping through windows. Omar and I sprint to Azura's front door, and I jog in place, ready to bolt if Mom comes out calling my name. Fortunately, Azura flings open her door before I can knock a second time and waves us in.

"What happened?" she gasps, closing the door behind us. Omar and I tell her about burying Cricket and the mini-tree growing at his grave and how I started twigging out.

I let go of my shirt cuffs. Thin branches explode into the foyer. The tingling sensation of growing has faded away, and it doesn't seem like I'm sprouting any new twigs or leaves. Took long enough. I start to break them off one by one. *Snnick. Snnick. Snick!*

Omar winces. "Doesn't that hurt?"

"Not really. Kinda like plucking a hair," I say. "A little pinch but not painful. Take this." I hand him a leafy stick. "I think it's stopped for now, but I've gotta get the rest of these off."

It takes five whole minutes to de-leaf. By the time I'm done, there's a nest of sticks and leaves surrounding me. I rub my skin. It's smooth. I relax. Everything seems normal again. Well, aside from my tree clippings littering the floor.

"What should we call you?" Omar asks. "You've got to have a cool name."

"What?" I'm not following.

"Your *superhero* name. How about Tree Boy? Or the Green Avenger? NO! TREE LORD."

Azura has her *um, NO* face on. "Yeaaaah. I think *Matteo* is fine."

"And let's get this straight—I'm *not* a superhero." I kick a stick across the room. "I don't want to be."

"Says every superhero *ever,*" Omar huffs.

Azura bends down, gathering branches and leaves in her arms. "Let's get these into the backyard. Don't want my dad asking questions."

Omar and I follow her out the back door with more

armfuls of sticks and leaves. Azura's yard has a pretty tall fence, so I don't think Mom'll be able to see us even if she tried.

The late-afternoon air is warm, almost summery. This time of year, the weather can't seem to make up its mind about what season it really is. I inhale deeply from a passing wind. Curls of hair flap against my forehead. I exhale. I'm still jittery but a little less than before.

We pile everything beneath a gnarled apple tree with limbs bent into almost-corners. White star blossoms glisten on the boughs. Someday those little flowers will be apples.

I wonder if that's what's happening to me. Am I budding? What'll I end up being when I finally bloom? A man or a tree? Or am I stuck being this weirdo bark-boy *thing* forever?

"You know, Matteo," Azura says, breaking me free of my worry spiral. "I think Omar's right."

He puffs up all proud of himself, but I repeat, "I am *not* a superhero."

"Oh, no, not about that," Azura agrees. Omar deflates. "But maybe this isn't a bad thing that's happening to you. He's right—it's cool."

"Totally FREAKING cool!" He twirls a stick into the air and catches it with his left hand.

I'm still pretty sure they're wrong, but now not one but *two* friends—including OMAR JONES—think I'm special.

A superhero, he called me. Maybe they're right and *I'm* wrong. What if I'm not a freak? What if I *am* gifted? Magical, even. Maybe this isn't a disease or something worse.

I let myself smile. "You guys really think so?"

They both nod enthusiastically.

"Why don't you try to do something?" Omar plops starry-eyed into the grass like I'm about to put on a magic show. "Like on purpose."

I flush. "You mean grow something?"

Azura crosses her legs next to Omar. "Yeah, give it a try. We'll help you. You said it happens when you lie, right?"

My eyes make their way back to Omar. There are things I've tried to keep hidden from him, but they want to come out. And maybe, deep down, I *want* them to. My fingers twitch at my sides. He hasn't abandoned me, even though I'm sure Tyler and Freddie would never let me live down treeing out. Azura hasn't left me either. They care. And I need help figuring out how to control whatever is happening, especially if my tears grow baby trees and it's not just an I-lied-and-my-body-didn't-like-it-so-I'm-growing-bark-and-leaves thing.

"Yeah," I say, trying to stay calm. "I think so."

"Wish something cool happened when I lie," Omar says. "I just get in trouble."

A mischievous gleam appears in Azura's eyes. "Do it. Tell a lie."

They stare at me. My toes curl in my shoes. "I don't know what to say."

"We can ask you questions," says Omar. "And you can tell us a lie."

Azura cracks her knuckles. "This'll be fun." She clears her throat. "Have you ever cheated on a test?"

"Nope!" I laugh awkwardly. "But wait, that's the truth. I meant yes!" Nothing happens. "Guess I messed that one up. Try again?"

"My turn," says Omar. He giggles. "Have you ever . . . eaten a booger?"

My face contorts. "Ew. Gross. No!"

Omar cackles, watching me closely. "Phew. Guess he's telling the truth."

"You're *supposed* to lie," Azura points out. "Hmm. Have you ever not brushed your teeth before going to school?"

She *knows* I've forgotten before. I asked her for a mint last week when I noticed how bad my breath stank. Confident in my lie, I say, "I always brush my teeth before school."

I wait for the tingle of growth, but nothing happens. "That's weird," I say. "It didn't work."

"Maybe it has to be a *real* lie, like something you're actually trying to hide," Omar says. Then he gets this look like he's cooked up something really devious. "Do you have a crush on someone?"

My mouth goes dry. Azura bites her lip because she

knows the truth and she's the only person in the world I've admitted it to. Against my better judgment, I say, "Nope."

My right fingertips stretch into branches. Curved leaves unfurl from tiny stems, and acorns bud in duos and trios. But for the first time, I watch with fascination instead of horror. *I'm* doing this. This is *me*. I laugh, wiggling my fingers, making the thin branches dance.

"DUDE! It worked!" Omar leaps up, taking my branching fingers in his hands. "These are the sickest fingernails I've ever seen."

I glow. "They're actually my fingers. I think."

His eyes widen, but he doesn't seem to put together that he's essentially holding my hand. That I can feel his skin on my bark and brushing my leaves.

"Wait," he says, still holding on. "So you *do* have a crush on someone?"

I will myself not to blush, but it's useless. Heat fills my cheeks. "I, uh—"

Azura saves the day, saying, "Okay, so whatever is happening to you, it's like the tree-ish stuff is holding you accountable. Like you can get away with lies that don't matter, but the real ones are a different story."

I groan. "My own body is punishing me for lying. This is totally unfair."

"Guess it'll keep you out of trouble?" Omar shrugs.

Azura goes on, her forehead wrinkling in concentration.

"But, like, could you grow *without* telling a lie? Have you tried?"

"Not yet," I say. I'm not sure how to explain the tree that grew over Cricket's grave, but maybe that was the oak doing the magic and not really me? I hold my hands out in front of me. "But I can give it a shot."

Omar crosses his arms, muttering, "I still want to know who you have a crush on." Then a mischievous look takes over his face, and he says, "Wait—is it . . . Azura?"

"What? No!" I say.

Azura laughs. "Um, definitely not."

This is getting dangerously close to being an actual mess. So I say, "You guys! Focus." I stare at my hands, mentally shoving all my attention and energy into them. "Aaaand . . . GROW!" I wave my hands around, but nothing happens.

"Not to be rude, but I don't think shouting 'grow' is gonna cut it." Azura says, "Maybe you have to *think* dishonest thoughts? Or, like, try lying to yourself?"

"I'll try." I close my eyes and focus on the itchy feeling of hiding the truth. I think about what I'm keeping from Omar and all the things I'm hiding from my parents. How Omar would totally jet if he knew I thought he was cute. How weirded out and disgusted my parents would be if they saw me grow bark. Shame and embarrassment creep around inside me.

My skin tingles and my eyes flash open. Bark creeps

up my wrist like the surface of a lake freezing over, and it doesn't stop until it reaches my elbow. "I did it!"

"Whoa! You've got tree armor!"

"Ha, yeah," I say, knocking on the wood shielding my skin.

Azura raises an eyebrow, but she's smiling. "So maybe there're still some questions about your tree powers, but we know it's got something to do with lying, and that it's definitely connected to the oak in Creekside Park. What's next?"

"We need to figure out how to stop it," I say. "Especially before my parents find out."

Omar's jaw drops. "Are you kidding me? You can't get rid of a superpower! It's awesome."

"Fine." I wiggle my twiggy fingers. "Maybe it is kind of awesome."

CREEKSIDE DOCUMENTARY TRANSCRIPT #19

SUBJECT: DONNA LORENZINI

· ·

DONNA LORENZINI

I loved sitting under that tree when I was a little girl. I'd bring a book and a bottle of iced tea and read for hours.

MATTEO LORENZINI

I didn't know that. Why there?

DONNA LORENZINI

I grew up in a loud house. Too loud most of the time. My parents, well . . . Creekside Park, that oak, it was my quiet escape. I was safe there.

TWENTY

Azura and Omar help me pry away the bark, sticks, and leaves before we part ways that afternoon. It's funny—it all seems to come off my skin a little easier with their help.

"You *could* tell your parents," Azura whispers in my ear before I leave. "They'll still love you, if that's what you're worried about."

Omar must overhear because he adds, "What's the worst that could happen?"

Of course, walking home I only think about the absolute worst possible things that could happen. They could be disgusted. They could be horrified. Maybe they wouldn't want me anymore. Maybe they'd send me somewhere, an asylum or hospital or some supersecret government center where they research boys with magical tree powers.

But when I get home, my worries fade into the smell of chicken, garlic, butter, and onions frying on the stovetop. Dad's in the kitchen, humming "That's Amore." He swirls a spoon in the popping pan, saying, "Making your favorite, kiddo: spaghetti with chicken and broccoli. How's that sound?"

My mouth waters. "Um, amazing? I'm starving." I hadn't realized how hungry I was until the smell of his cooking hit me full force.

Mom welcomes me with a hug and a kiss on each cheek. "You're late," she says.

"Sorry."

"Homework right away after dinner, okay?" she says. Then she leans in, voice lilting. "But more important . . . how were things with Omar?"

"Fine," I say quickly. I slide my hands into my pockets, remembering the feeling of him holding my barky hand. "Good, actually. Really good."

Dad brings over a spoon with a piece of chicken coated in sauteed onions, butter, and garlic. "Omar, huh? Wasn't sure you two were still friends." He holds the spoon to my mouth. "Taste test."

Steam rises off the food. The chicken's perfectly golden brown. I blow on it and gobble it down. "Oh my god. That's so good." I wipe my lips. "Yeah, Omar and I are better now."

"Great to hear," Dad says. "I've always liked that kid."

Mom grins. "Me too. Such a sweetheart. He's a good fit for you."

"Uh, yeah." I nod. I know she means he's a good fit *as*

a friend, but part of me wonders if she can tell how I really feel about Omar. Oh God. That would be so embarrassing. I hope not.

Dad goes back to humming as he finishes prepping dinner. Mom hands me three plates to set the table. She starts humming along with Dad, and then I do too. Then our humming becomes belting out, "When the moon hits your eye like a big pizza pie, that's amore!" Dad grabs Mom around the waist and spins her around. Then they drag me in, and we're all dancing around like total goofballs. But in this moment, everything feels right.

This is what I want my life to be. It's too good to ruin with tree superpowers.

I'm better off keeping my secrets to myself.

The next morning, Azura and I get to school early. The hallways are echoey without all the other students filling every inch of space. Not even all the fluorescent lights are on. A few teachers eye us strangely as they sip their coffee. *It's way too early for kids*, their shadowed eyes seem to say before they disappear into classrooms.

"You think he'll be here?" I ask.

"He's *old*," says Azura. "He'll be here. Dad says the older he gets, the earlier his internal clock goes off."

I stick out my tongue. "Ugh. That sounds terrible. I don't want to get old."

When we walk into the library, the smell of musty books rushes my senses. There's a new display near the circulation desk featuring books from authors who are Black, Indigenous, or people of color. Mr. Kowalski stands in front of it, arranging and rearranging a trio of books I read last year. When the floor creaks beneath our feet, his head turns our way.

"Oh! Early birders," he says. "What brings you to my domain this bright morn? Interested in a new book?"

Azura tucks a strand of blue hair behind her ear. "Uh, no, sorry."

Mr. Kowalski sighs. "A man can hope." He sets the final book on the display. "Well then. What can I do ya for?"

"We, um, have a kind of weird question to ask you," Azura says, nudging me forward.

The old librarian smiles, folding his hands on the pouch of his stomach. Today he's wearing a fuzzy yellow sweater. "Well, lay it on me."

I clear my throat. "Did you—um, did you ever go by a nickname? Kaz, maybe?"

Mr. Kowalski's expression shifts in slow motion, from flat to startled to something like waking up after sleeping in on a Sunday morning. "No one's called me that in years," he says. He tilts his head, grinning. "Where did you hear that?"

I can't believe it. Azura was right. It *is* him.

"We read it, actually," she says.

"Can't imagine it's written in many places beyond an old yearbook or two." Mr. Kowalski adjusts his glasses. "Where did you find it?"

Azura and I exchange a glance. "A tree," I say. "The old oak in Creekside Park."

A hazy look comes over him. He thumbs his nose. "Like on a piece of paper? Or did someone vandalize the tree? I can't—"

"No, nothing like that," says Azura. "But we were wondering, do the initials *LL* mean anything to you?"

His face falls. "Excuse me?"

"Like the letters." She tries again, overenunciating: "EL-EL."

He waves his hand at her. "No, no, I heard you." His hand clutches his chest. "That was—I just—I wasn't expecting . . . You saw this? On the tree? Kaz and LL together?"

We nod.

He sniffs. Clears his throat once, twice. His sweater rises and falls on his chest in growing waves. I'm worried he's about to be sick.

"Are you okay, Mr. Kowalski?" I ask.

His head shakes, but he says, "Fine. I'll be fine. I just need some water."

He reaches for his cane, which was resting against the counter, and shuffles past us, behind the circulation desk, and through a doorway into his office. The door closes behind him without another word. We wait. When he doesn't come back out, Azura asks if we should knock.

"Maybe not," I say. "I think—I think he needs space right now."

"What if he's sick?" she says. "Or hurt."

There's a weird feeling in my gut. "No. I think we should leave him alone for now. I think . . . I think he's sad."

"Why?" Azura asks. "Because of the tree? Is it LL? Is it both?"

"I'm not sure." I chew my lip as I think. "We should see what else we can find about LL. Maybe they're the initials of a family member or a woman he loved or something like that?"

Azura shrugs. "Maybe? We can do more research on the tree too, how it really got here and all that. I don't know how it's all connected, but I think we're on the right track."

"I think so too." And that kind of terrifies me. Much as I want to know what's happening to me, I'm worried about what we'll find. Given Mr. Kowalski's reaction, it could be something terrible—something that's meant to stay hidden.

The first bell rings, and we exit the library. More kids are in the hallway now.

"LL's gotta be someone important," Azura goes on. "What if we need to find them next? Or maybe we were supposed to find them first? What if we just messed everything up by talking to Mr. Kowalski?"

"Maybe," I say, "but I don't know how we'll find out who LL is *without* Mr. Kowalski. LL could literally be anyone."

A voice calls loudly behind us, making us both jump.

"HEY!" Omar bounds down the hallway, his backpack slapping against him. He eyes my arms. "Anything *interesting* going on this morning?"

I hug my torso and pick my next words carefully. He might know about me, but I'm not sure I'm ready for him to know *everything*. "Just talking with Mr. Kowalski," I say.

"The librarian?" He hikes his backpack up on his shoulders. "He's kinda cranky, isn't he? He was always on my brother about late fines. And making videos when he should have been reading. What'd he want with you?"

I don't even have to lie. "Nothing."

CREEKSIDE DOCUMENTARY TRANSCRIPT #20

SUBJECT: SAMANTHA GRAINGER

. . . .

SAMANTHA GRAINGER

Yeah, I know the tree. Used to catch fireflies in the park with my little brother. The brightest ones are always buzzing around that old oak.

MATTEO LORENZINI

Why do you think there're so many stories about the tree?

SAMANTHA GRAINGER

I don't know. I guess trees are kind of an enigma. We can't really know what they're thinking or feeling, so we make it up.

MATTEO LORENZINI

So you think the stories aren't true?

SAMANTHA GRAINGER

As a social studies teacher, I like to remind students that history, really, is just stories we tell about the past. We often take history as truth but forget that the storyteller matters just as much as the story itself. What is their truth? Is it the same as someone else's? (Laughs) I guess that's my longwinded way of saying, who knows?

TWENTY-ONE

Azura and I had to tackle the Mr. Kowalski situation early this morning because today our social studies teacher, Ms. Grainger, is taking us to one of her "all-time favorite places." This place? Creekside Cemetery. Cue the entire sixth grade's side-eye, including mine.

Ms. Grainger leads us out of Creekside Middle School and through downtown Creekside. She's a petite white woman with dark brown hair pulled into a ponytail. It's not quite seventy degrees, but the sun's solo in the blue sky and a warm breeze picks up every few seconds. If you ask me, it's a little too cheery for a visit to a bunch of dead people.

Creekside Cemetery is hidden behind Good Christian Church on the west end of town. We're in a local history unit, and Ms. Grainger tasked us with finding five tombstones with epitaphs (these short sayings carved into the headstones) that we think are interesting. We're supposed to research each person when we get back to school. Unfortunately, she splits us into groups, and to my horror, I end up with Tyler Sudbury and Freddie McCoy.

"Maybe it won't be as bad as you think," Omar says as he trails behind Maisy Patel and Edwina Worst up the hill of gray headstones.

"But I—" A heavy arm lands on my shoulder.

Tyler's nacho-cheese breath clouds around me as he says, "We got this. Right, wuss?"

"Don't call me that." I try to shrug free, but he pulls me in tighter.

"Someone's cranky," he says, mocking me. "You scared?"

With a final yank, I stumble away, and my knee collides with Johnnie Johnson's tombstone. GAH! My fingers clench into fists as I try to hide the pain. "Let's just get this over with," I manage through gritted teeth.

"All good over there?" Ms. Grainger's sunglasses descend over the bridge of her nose.

Tyler shoots finger guns at her. "We're cool, we're cool."

She looks wearily at Tyler and then saunters off to another group hovering around a tall headstone with a floral design framing the edges.

I can't decide if I'm more relieved or annoyed that she straight up ignored the fact that Tyler was bullying me. Eager to get this over with, I rush through the field of tombstones that look like rows of crooked teeth. Some are so worn that the engravings are hard to make out. I stop at one with tiny angels floating in the corners. Tyler and Freddie skulk behind me.

I pass by headstone after headstone, noting names and epitaphs: Larry Henderson ("Convinced of UFOs till the end."); Sylvia Pesternach ("I regret nothing."); Millie Mae Edgerton ("This is not an epitaph."). Freddie and Tyler totally ignore my suggestions, which makes me want to scream, but then my eye catches a name on a stone and I almost forget about them entirely.

I read out loud. "Lisa Lemon." *LL*. Just like the initials in the tree, the ones that pointed us to Mr. Kowalski. Is *this* who we're looking for?

"What are you doing?" Freddie says.

"Quiet." I kneel, doing some mental math based on when she was born and when she died. Numbers click into place. Lisa Lemon passed before I was born but not too long before. And if she were alive today, she'd probably be as old as Mr. Kowalski. Then I look farther down at her epitaph and my heart races. The epitaph reads: "The strongest trees have the deepest roots."

I'm all shivers. There's even mention of a tree in her epitaph! Lisa Lemon *has* to be the answer! After all the interviews we've done with Creeksiders, there's no doubt in my mind that this isn't a coincidence. I pop up. I've got to tell Azura.

But Tyler gets in my way. "Are you gonna write down what it says or make out with it?"

Freddie snickers.

"Why would I make out with a tombstone?" I say, blushing at the ridiculous words.

"I don't know. You're the weirdo." Tyler scuffs the grass. "Ugh. I'm bored."

Freddie says, "Matteo, you find the best ones and let us know when you're done."

"We're supposed to do it together," I say. "It's a *group* project."

"Right." Tyler smirks. "*We're* a group, and *you'll* do the project."

I'm so freaking tired of him acting like he's better than everyone else. What I wouldn't give to put him in his place, just once. Make *him* feel small or weak. If I had some way to—

Oh.

My eyes flit to the branches of a nearby tree. Maybe I *do* have a way to get him back. I flex my hands. An idea forms. A slightly-evil-but-superawesome-super*powered idea.*

Quickly, I scribble down Lisa Lemon's name and the line about the tree, and then I put on my most sincere smile and point to the crab apple tree a few graves down. "Fine. I'll get it done and meet you over there. Happy?"

Tyler finger guns me. "Knew you'd come around, wuss."

Wuss. My brain screams like Mom's teapot. Wouldn't surprise me if actual steam funneled out of my nostrils. But I say, "Totally. I've got you."

Which is true.

And now to put my lying skills to the test.

Tyler and Freddie wander off, "parkouring" (they actually shout the word each time they jump) off tombstones toward the crab apple tree until Ms. Grainger yells at them to stop being disrespectful. I, meanwhile, focus on all the lies I'm keeping. How I'm hiding the truth about my tree powers from Mom and Dad. That shame and embarrassment that helped me tree out the other day in Azura's backyard. Only this time, nothing happens. *Come on. Work!* I concentrate harder on all the other things I'm not telling them: how bad Tyler really makes me feel, how annoyed I am whenever Dad compares me to another boy my age, how I feel like I'll never be good enough. Still, I don't grow. Frustrated, I pace around the headstones, muttering every lie that comes to mind.

"The sky is green."

"I'm six feet tall."

"Ms. Grainger is the nicest teacher at school."

But nothing happens. I wiggle my fingers. *Grow already!* I kneel behind a tombstone, staring at my hands. *Do something!* I rack my brain for better lies. *Lie* lies. More *honest* lies. I glance over at Omar, who's kneeling in front of a pillar that reminds me of the Washington Monument. He says something, and Maisy and Edwina giggle. A pang of jealousy makes my feet twitch. I want to be over there. With them. With Omar.

And that's when I realize my very honest lie. A truth I haven't even really admitted to myself. I say the words out loud because I need this to work.

"I do not have a crush on Omar Jones," I whisper to myself. I get hot all over with embarrassment, which tells me it's working. "I do not have a have a crush on Omar Jones. I do not have a—"

Bark scabs my fingernails and crawls over my knuckles. I grin. "That's more like it."

Graveyards are eerie, even in sunshine. Ghosts and creepy things come to mind. If anyone deserves to be haunted by a malevolent spirit (or tree boy), it's Tyler Sudbury. I snicker and sink my barky fingers into the soil. *Roots*, I think. *Grow roots.*

Nothing happens at first, but then, a few tombstones away, an earthworm of brown root pokes through the grass. It flails like an alien tentacle. I almost laugh out loud. *YES. This is perfect.* Now to get it all the way over to the crab apple tree a few graves down . . .

The root nubbin plunges back into the soil. Adrenaline and lies course through my veins and into the earth. I'm shaking I'm so excited. I repeat my dishonest mantra like a spell: *I don't have a crush on Omar Jones. I don't have a crush on Omar Jones.* My roots home in on Tyler and Freddie, weaving around stones and coffins. I watch from behind my headstone.

Tyler and Freddie are chucking pebbles at the trunk of the crab apple, completely unaware of the roots that emerge behind them. I chuckle. This is going to be awesome. My roots creep forward, poke the boys' calves, and duck back underground.

Freddie whips around. "What was that?"

Tyler scans the cemetery, and I pretend like I'm totally fascinated by the epitaph on the headstone in front of me. "Probably a bug," I hear him say. "You scared?"

"No," Freddie retorts. "You are." He hurls an acorn-size rock at the tree.

When they go back to chucking pebbles, I spin my lies some more. *Shoom!* Roots fly out, smack the backs of their heads, and vanish once again. Tyler and Freddie howl in unison, rubbing their skulls.

"You hit me!" Tyler shouts.

Freddie scowls. "Dude, *you* hit *me*!"

"Liar! I didn't hit you."

While they bicker, my roots slither up and tap them each on the shoulder. Tyler and Freddie spin around in opposite directions, but there's nothing to see. I make sure of that. But their confused expressions are priceless. I have to stop myself from laughing out loud.

"Dude, how did you—"

Tyler shakes his head. "It wasn't me." Now he pales, realization dawning on his face. He warily scans the headstones. I duck lower. He inches closer to Freddie. "You don't think it was . . ."

Freddie shakes his head. "Dude, don't you dare say a ghost. I hate ghosts."

"I wasn't. I mean, they're not real," Tyler scoffs. "Right?"

"Definitely not," says Freddie, but he doesn't sound even half-convinced.

My roots lash out one last time, flicking their behinds with a sharp *crack*.

"AHHHHHH!"

Tyler and Freddie bolt to Ms. Grainger, and I double over with laughter behind my tombstone. Ms. Grainger takes her glasses off, perplexed, and shouts with surprise when Freddie throws his arms around her. "It's paranormal activity!" he cries. "IT'S PARANORMAL ACTIVITY! I DON'T WANT TO DIE."

"Get! Off! Me!" Ms. Grainger says, prying him from her. Tyler, meanwhile, has maneuvered around her, making sure she stands between him and the crab apple tree. He's whiter than a pair of clean underwear.

I wipe tears from my eyes. Oh my God. This was better than I ever could have imagined. Omar's right—I *do* have superpowers. Lying is my superstrength! I'll take down all the bullies, one branch at a time.

"That's enough, that's enough!" Ms. Grainger shouts, shushing Tyler's and Freddie's whining. "Class, that's it! This field trip is *over*! We're done!"

I pull my fingers from the dirt, snapping them free of roots. I brush off the crusts of bark and smile to myself. Yes, my work here is most definitely done.

CREEKSIDE DOCUMENTARY TRANSCRIPT #21

SUBJECT: VINCENZO LORENZINI

. . . .

VINCENZO LORENZINI
You know I had my first kiss under that oak.

MATTEO LORENZINI
Ew, gross.

VINCENZO LORENZINI
It was your mom.

MATTEO LORENZINI
Oh. Still gross.

TWENTY-TWO

Omar smirks at me on our walk home from school. "That was you today. Wasn't it?"

"What?" I say, playing it cool.

Azura rolls her eyes at me. "Tyler and Freddie flipping out at the cemetery. It had to be you."

I act innocent, enjoying this game of keeping my super-hero identity secret. "Maybe it was, maybe it wasn't."

Omar leans in to whisper, "It was hilarious. They were seriously spooked."

But Azura says, "What if they caught you? Then your secret would be out. Did you think about that?"

I shrug, refusing to give her any of the high ground. "I have no idea what you're talking about." A leaf unfurls from the tip of my nose. Their jaws drop like broken nutcrackers. My hands fly to my face. I pluck the leaf and fling it to the ground. "Oops."

Azura purses her lips. "That's right. Don't get cocky."

Omar tucks his thumbs under the shoulder straps of his backpack. "Well, I still think it was cool. Whatever you did or didn't do, you totally showed Tyler who's boss."

And that's all I need to hear before I'm grinning from ear to ear.

At the end of the street, Omar splits off from our trio to head home, and then it's just me and Azura. She walks closer, her voice quieting. "Have you thought about this morning? About what we're going to do next about LL?"

"Oh, that's right!" Our talk with Mr. Kowalski feels like it happened a million years ago. Pulling one over on Tyler and Freddie is all I've thought about since it happened. I almost forgot about what I found at the graveyard today. I pull out my notebook. "I got the answer! I found LL in the cemetery. Her name was Lisa Lemon." I show Azura the epitaph I wrote down. "See? She's gotta be the one!"

Azura brightens. "No way!" Then she scowls. "But if she's dead, how does that help us?"

"Maybe someone else can tell us about her. Then we can figure out how she's connected to Mr. Kowalski and the tree."

"Her name is kind of familiar. Maybe someone talked about her in our documentary interviews." She grins at her own idea. "Yeah, let me look back at our recordings. Dad's going on another date with Ms. Geraldo, so I'll have lots of time tonight. I'll see if I can find anything."

"Sounds good to me."

We reach the sidewalk outside our front yards, and she hesitates. "Have you told your parents yet? About what you can do?"

I don't get why she won't let this go. "No. And I don't plan to."

"But—"

"Azura, stop. My parents will only make things worse if they find out. They have zero chill. They're not like your dad."

She frowns. "My dad's not always chill, and you can't keep it from them forever."

"I'll take however long I can get." I cross my arms over my chest. "Especially if I can make the tree stuff go away. We just have to solve the whole Mr. Kowalski and Lisa Lemon mystery before my body gets totally out of control."

She looks upset. "I just want what's best for you." Then she gives me a small smile. "Have a good night then. See you tomorrow?"

"Yeah, see you tomorrow." But I don't smile at her. Why does she have to spoil a perfectly good day?

As I'm crawling into bed that night, Dad pops his head through my door. "Hey, sport."

I sit up, propping my pillow behind me. "What's up?"

He scratches the back of his head. "I just—I wanted to see how you're doing. Your mom and I, we know you've been having a tough time lately."

I feel out each word carefully on my tongue before I speak. "Baseball's just been harder than I thought it would be. Tyler's annoying, but I'll get through it."

He sits on the corner of the bed. "We're gonna talk to Coach Mathis at tomorrow's game about how Tyler's been treating you. I heard him giving you a hard time at your last practice."

I lunge forward. "No! Don't. *Please.* That'll just make things worse. I can handle it."

"You shouldn't have to handle it."

"But I can," I say, thinking back to the cemetery. "I will."

Dad doesn't look too convinced, but he says, "You're sure?"

"I'm sure."

"You know it's my job to protect you, right? I—" He scratches the side of his nose with his thumb. "I want to do for you what my dad never did for me."

I sit up taller. He means well and I know being a good dad is important to him, especially since Grandpa wasn't around, but this isn't about him. I can take care of myself. "I don't need protecting from Tyler Sudbury," I say.

His fingers spider back and forth over my blanket. I wait, knowing there's more he wants to say. Finally, he goes on, but his tone is a little softer. "I *know* you, Matteo."

"I mean, yeah, I know," I say, laughing nervously. "I *am* your son."

He looks to the ceiling and then back at me. "What I mean is that I know when something's up with you. You're my *everything*. I feel like—I mean, you know you can tell your mom and me anything, don't you?"

My tongue becomes sandpaper against the roof of my mouth. I think about all the secrets I've been keeping. About Omar and my weird superpowers and now this whole thing with Lisa Lemon and Mr. Kowalski and who knows what else we're going to find. But I say, really, really hoping it's true, "Yeah, I know."

When I don't grow, I relax a little. I guess that just because you *can* tell someone anything, it doesn't mean you always *have* to.

He grips my knee. "So is there anything you want to tell me?"

I sigh with relief because this will definitely be the truth. "Nope. I'm good." *Nothing I* want *to tell you*. I smile. "I promise."

His lips slide to the side of his face, still looking unconvinced. "If you say so." He stands to leave. "But if you change your mind, I'm here. Your mom too."

I groan. "Don't worry about me. Seriously."

Dad breaks his solemn mood and grins. "All right, sport. Sleep tight, 'kay?"

"Yeah. You too."

"Love you, kid." He pulls the door closed behind him.

"Love you too," I call after him.

I slip under the blankets, more confident about my ability to sidestep the truth. And after all the lies the past couple weeks, I think I really was just honest with Dad. I *can* handle myself, and tomorrow I'm going to prove it.

CREEKSIDE DOCUMENTARY TRANSCRIPT #22

SUBJECT: COACH MATHIS

. . . .

COACH MATHIS

Stories about the tree? Let's see. I heard once that it got struck by lightning.

MATTEO LORENZINI

That's it?

COACH MATHIS

Yeah. I mean, they say a whole giant branch came down.

MATTEO LORENZINI

Cool.

TWENTY-THREE

The next morning, I'm not one bit nervous about our game against the Crimson Snakes. You see, I'm not the same boy I was the first two games: helpless, worthless, useless. Now that I'm getting my body to work *for* me, I'm not *less* anything.

I'm *more*.

And I know just how to prove it to Mom and Dad, Coach Mathis, and Tyler. On my way out, I snag our family baseball bat that's leaning against my dresser. I still don't fully understand how the oak and the bat and me are all connected, but today, I'm making the magic work *for* me, just like I did in the cemetery. And I don't care what lies I've got to tell to do it.

It's sunny and warm. Perfect baseball weather. The field behind Creekside Middle School is freshly cut. The smell tickles my nose. Off in the distance, the whir and thwack of a riding mower fills the air.

Omar and I stretch near the dugout. He reaches for his toes but tilts his head toward me. "Those Snakes don't look *that* tough."

I glance at the opposing team, rolling my shoulders forward. The Crimson Snakes have the best record in our little league circuit, but they're scrawny. Only like one kid on their team is tall, and he seems more interested in playing with pill bugs in the grass than throwing a ball.

I roll my shoulders back. "We can take 'em."

Omar bends into a lunge. "You think you'll get a hit?"

"I don't think so," I say, eyeing their pencil-armed pitcher. "I *know* I will."

He lunges to the other side, beaming. "That's what I like to hear."

To hide the red creeping into my cheeks, I fold in half and reach for my toes. Blood rushes to my ears, masking my blush. Gravity for the win!

"Gather 'round," Coach Mathis calls. "Huddle up!"

We join the other Blue Whales in the circle, our arms weaving around each other's shoulders. Tyler stands across from me, but it's like he doesn't even see me, so I stare him down until he catches my eye. He gives me a weird look, but I want him to remember me glaring at him when I send that ball soaring over left field.

"Now I know what you're thinking," Coach Mathis says. "These Snakes might look like tater tots, but let me tell you, they're fresh out of the oven and coming in hot. I'm good friends with their coach, and he's no joker. You kids think *I'm* tough. Phew!" He takes off his cap and wipes his forehead. "Don't let your guard down, now, you hear? If we win today, it'll be because you all fought for it. You ready to get this?"

My teammates mumble a half-hearted "sure," but I shout, "Yeah!" Everyone looks at me like I suddenly grew a second head. Coach Mathis seems surprised by my enthusiasm too, but he says, "That's the spirit, Matteo. Now let's try this again. ARE YOU READY TO WIN?"

The other guys look at each other warily. Omar glances at me, and I give him my most confident smile. He smiles back. Our grinning seems to spread around the circle. Even Tyler and Freddie look more confident. Our shoulders rise as we inhale, and together we shout, "YEAAAH!!!"

A crackle of energy zips through us that wasn't there before. *Because of me*, I think. I *did that*. Coach Mathis beams. He gives me a wink, like we're in on a secret together. My chest puffs out. I like this feeling, like I'm king of the Blue Whales. This must be how Tyler feels all the time. I could get used to this.

"Now that's what I'm talking 'bout," Coach Mathis says. He puts his hand in the center of the circle. My hand flies on top of Coach's, and the other boys pile on. "On the count of three, 'Whales will win.' One. Two. THREE!"

"WHALES WILL WIN!"

Our circle breaks up. I grab my glove and jog out to left field. The morning sun heats the back of my neck. Beneath my shoes, I can sense the earth. Blades of grass, a ladybug flitting from one to the next. Maybe it's my secret super-powers (or that, for once, I'm kind of comfortable in my own skin), but it's like I'm connected to all of it: the field, the team, even Creekside. For the first time in a long time, I feel like I really, truly belong.

My good vibes waver, though, when the first Snake to bat, a Black boy with midnight-colored skin, smashes the ball into right field. He lands on second base before the ball makes it back to Tyler on the mound. Even from so far away, I can tell Tyler's ticked. He stares down the next batter like the kid dissed his mom. I grin. It's a nice break to have someone else on the receiving end of his attitude.

The next batter makes contact on the second pitch. The ball sails over Tyler's head. Omar calls it, and the ball lands in his glove. The Blue Whales' fans, my parents included, erupt in cheers. I know Omar wishes his brother were here to see that catch, but only his parents are sitting in the stands. I whoop especially loud for him, hoping it might make up for it.

The next batter is the one tall kid on the Crimson Snakes' team. He's Latino and has reddish-brown skin. He spits into the dirt at home plate and hunkers down with the bat at his shoulder. His face is all business. Something in my gut tells me to get ready.

A second later, I find out why. He hits Tyler's first pitch, and the ball flies right for me. My knees rattle, but I steady myself. I raise my glove, one eye focused on the incoming shadow, the other squinting against the sun. I step back, one, two, three steps. I shift my glove a little to the left. The ball eclipses the sun. I'm pretty sure I've forgotten how to breathe.

Please let me catch this, please let me catch this, please let me catch this.

It's so close now.

So close . . .

FWUMP!

I scream with glee. I caught it! My palm burns, and I pump the air. "YES!" I hurl the ball back to Tyler, who looks at me with a little less disdain than he normally does.

"GO MATTEOOO!" Mom and Dad scream from the stands. I do my best to ignore them, but I also secretly love this moment. This is what I want. To make them proud. To be the son they always wanted. I sneak a glance at Omar too. Did he see what I just did?

A hummingbird beats against the inside of my rib cage. He's grinning in my direction. That whole dimpled smile feels like it was made just for me. I swell with pride. I'm doing this. *I am in control.* Maybe I don't need the family bat or tree magic after all. Maybe I can get a hit all on my own.

I ride high on that feeling until the bottom of the fifth inning, when it's time for me to bat. Because that's just my luck, the bases are loaded, and Jeremy Kosta just got us our second out. Tyler's up after me, of course, and he audibly groans when he realizes our hopes for this inning rest in my hands. My nerves can't handle the pressure. My hands are trembling and I'm not even at home plate yet.

But this means I absolutely need whatever help I can get. I ditch my aluminum bat, unzip my gear bag, and pull out my secret weapon. *I'm special,* I tell myself. *I can do things no other boy can.* I firmly grip our family bat. Today is my day.

"Where are you going with that?" Coach Mathis points to the wooden bat in my hands.

"Up to bat?"

Coach holds out an aluminum bat. "Not with that. Regulation bats only."

My stomach drops. This bat is the only chance I have at getting us through this inning. I just know it. "Please. Just this once."

"Rules are rules," says Coach. "Give it here."

"But—" A million responses tangle in my brain, some true . . . some not so true. I need to say whatever will get him to let me use the bat, even if that means I tree out. "Please, it was my dad's bat and my grandpa's before that."

True. "I told Dad I'd do this for him, in honor of my grandpa. Please, it would mean so much to him." *Not so true.* I feel something sprout in my hair. I smash my hat down, hoping Coach doesn't think anything of it.

His stern expression slips. "Matteo, I can't—"

"Please. Just this one time. Dad asked me to. It'll mean the world to him." *Definitely not true.*

Now my feet tingle. Uh-oh. My shoes suddenly feel a little tighter. I'm sure my socks are going to be full of leaves when I get home.

"Fine," Coach finally relents. "Just this once. For your dad."

I almost hug him—*almost.* "Thank you. Thank you so much."

I jog to home plate and grind my feet into the dirt. The itch of my lies slithers up my shins. But I can work the tree magic in my favor. *Come on, superpowers. Help me out here.* I imagine bark growing under my jersey and down my arms, giving me superstrength. I mean, it hasn't before, but if I focus hard enough, maybe . . .

The Crimson Snakes' pitcher is a pale girl with long blond hair in two dangling braids. A spray of red-brown freckles dots her cheeks. She winds up for the first pitch.

I inhale, reminding myself to exhale as the ball flies at me.

I am in control, I am in control, I am in—

"Strike one," the umpire shouts. The catcher throws the ball back to the pitcher.

Crap. I didn't think this through. Superstrength won't matter if I can't actually *hit* the ball. *Come on, Matteo. Just hit. The. BALL.*

Tyler and a couple of the other guys grumble. I don't look back. I don't care what they say. I can do this. I tighten my grip. *Come on, bat. Come on, body. Do something!*

Mom shouts, "You've got this, Matteo!"

Then Dad, "Just like we practiced!"

In comes the second pitch, and this time the ball hits the tip of the bat and goes foul. A second strike, but I have one more chance. That's all I need. I know it.

I'm special. I'm powerful. I'm not who they think I am.

I'm not a loser.

I'm as good as any of them.

The Crimson Snake hurls the ball. My eyes don't leave the white blur for a millisecond. The bat whips forward and—*CRACK!*

The ball is in the air. It climbs, and I can hardly believe what I'm seeing. Was that magic, or was that me? I mean, I hoped I could do it, but now that it's happened, I'm frozen in delight.

Then Coach Mathis shouts, "RUN!"

I snap out of my daze and blast off to first base. I'm half-way there when I realize I'm still holding the bat. I was so shocked and excited I forgot to drop it back at home plate. I open my hand to let it fall.

There's just one problem. It's stuck. I try to unwrap my fingers from the handle, but my skin is fused to it. I try to shake it off. The bat just whips around. The first baseman backs out of the way, hands raised in surrender. I stop, trying to tear the bat free, but everyone is shouting for me to keep running, and I realize I hit the ball THAT FAR. Who cares if it's stuck to me?! I book it to second, the bat flailing at my side.

As I come to a stop, the second baseman gives me a weird look. I glance down. My stomach crawls up my throat. *Oh no, oh no, oh no.* I went too far. The bat's *growing.* Twigs and leaves and little branches poke in every direction from the barrel. I can hide my tree-ish growth under my clothes, but I can't hide this!

"No, no, no! Not NOW!" I thrash around some more, but the bat won't let go of me. Bits of tree sprout from the handle. Forking twigs and little green leaves. A cluster of acorns. Then the back of *my hand* sprouts, then my wrist, then my forearm.

I want the ground to swallow me whole. The baseball field's gone silent, but I can feel everyone's eyes on me. I should have known this wouldn't work. I'm such an idiot!

Every second they stare feels like a lifetime, and I live and die every single one. My humiliation and embarrassment multiply with each new breath I take. My lungs stutter in my chest. Each inhale gets sharper, harder. Black fog creeps in on the edges of my vision. White spots dot the field. This wasn't part of the plan. This isn't how it was supposed to go.

Real boys don't do this.

Real boys get doubles because they're talented. *Because they're* strong.

Not because they're liars. Not because they grow.

So I run, and I don't stop, even when they call my name. I run as fast as my legs will go.

CREEKSIDE DOCUMENTARY TRANSCRIPT #23

SUBJECT: MATTEO LORENZINI

. . . .

AZURA GONZALEZ

What do you think, Matteo? Do you believe what they say about the tree in Creekside Park?

MATTEO LORENZINI

Honestly, I don't know what to believe anymore.

TWENTY-FOUR

Dad and Mom chase after me, but I'm too fast for them.

They find me on the floor in my bedroom, still in my baseball uniform, surrounded by leaves and twigs. The baseball bat, no longer in my grasp, lies on the carpet. It's almost unrecognizable. The grip is gnarled and knotted except for where my hand was. There's a perfect outline of my palm and fingers. The barrel is now the trunk of a miniature tree. Green leaves and thin branches hide the once-smooth surface. The polish from all those decades of Lorenzini hands is ruined because of me.

I really thought I could control my powers. I was getting better at managing the lies and making them work for me, but now everything's a bigger mess than before.

Mom drops next to me. "Matteo! What happened? Are you okay?"

I shrink away. "I—I'm fine."

Her fingers run over the back of my hand, and then she turns it over to examine my palm and each individual finger. "That was such an incredible hit. But the bat— I could have sworn your hand was glued to the thing." She laughs nervously. "I was worried you'd be full of splinters."

I pull my hand back. "No, it's—that's not what happened."

Dad picks up the sprouted bat from the ground. "What in the world *did* happen? How does dead wood start growing again?"

I'm not ready to tell them, but I don't know how I can keep the truth from them now. UGH. This is what I get for thinking I got away with hiding my secrets from Dad last night. I search their faces. They both look so concerned. Maybe being forced to tell them is a good thing. If I'm being honest with myself, I probably never would have felt ready to tell them. And maybe Azura's been right all along. Maybe I need to tell Mom and Dad the truth, and maybe it'll be okay. I let out a heavy sigh. Then I say, "It's complicated."

Dad looks at me. "What does that mean? Do you know what happened? Did—did you have something to do with this?"

"I—"

But I can hardly get a word out before Mom cuts him off. "Don't be ridiculous. Of course he didn't. How could he? I'm just glad there's nothing *wrong*. Stop fussing with that bat, Vin." She beams at me. "We need to celebrate you getting your first hit! And a *double!*"

My intestines knot up. Is she being serious? How doesn't she see there's a problem? Is she choosing *not* to see what's really going on, or is she really that unaware? I mean, there's a magically growing bat right under her nose! If I tell her the truth, will she even listen?

But Dad doesn't let up. "Matteo, what aren't you telling us? We can help you."

His voice isn't stern, and his tone is genuine. Yet I still have worms crawling in my stomach. If I tell him, maybe he'll help me convince Mom that something *is* happening to me, but that I'm okay. Maybe I made a mistake not being honest with him last night. Maybe he'll see that something is *right* with me the way Omar and Azura do. Like I'm magic or a superhero.

"Dad's right," I finally manage. "There is something I haven't been telling you." My eyes ping-pong between them, trying to gauge their level of freak-out. Slowly I say, "It *was* me. I made the bat grow."

"Honey, don't be silly." Mom laughs. "That's impossible."

I sigh. "I know. It's totally bananas, but over the past few weeks, some weird things have been going on. I didn't know how to tell you before."

Dad sets the bat down. "What do you mean 'weird'?" He sits on the floor across from me. "Bud, you can tell us."

What happens if they don't react the way I want them to? I mean, it's not like I have a choice now. I'm already in the middle of telling them. They're going to react however they want. I know they love me, but I'm still scared.

I take a deep breath in, and then I *almost* come out with it. "I've always felt a little different from people, but lately it's been more than that. A lot more."

"Which is totally normal for a boy your age," Mom says quickly, her tone sparkling.

"That's not what I mean," I say. "When I say I'm not like the other kids, I mean it. I—I *grow*. Not just like, getting taller or hair under my arms. I *grow* grow. Leaves and twigs and bark." They stare at me in silence. "Like a tree."

"Very funny." Mom laughs. She pokes my ribs. "You got us."

"I'm serious," I say.

"Matteo, that's just not possible," she says. "Cut the jokes. What's really going on?"

I cringe. "I'm not joking."

Dad leans forward. "Bud, you gotta give us more to go on."

"I don't know what you want me to say!" I almost shout. "I'm turning into a tree! And it's kind of cool. Sometimes it's leaves, sometimes it's bark. Omar and Azura, they think I—"

Dad's hands go up. "Matteo, that's not what I meant. Your mom's right. You're not turning into a tree, but if you think something's wrong, we can have Dr. Wilson—"

"You're not listening!" I stand up. "Ask me a question."

"What?" They say in unison.

"Ask me a question. One that you think I might lie about."

They exchange a glance. Then Mom folds her hands in her lap and says, "Okay. I'll play." She squints like she's thinking up a really clever question. With a sly grin, she slowly asks, "What's *really* going on between you and Omar?"

My jaw drops, but I shut it quickly. I try not to let my leg twitch. I don't know what question I was expecting, but that was so not it. The good news is they don't know how my superpowers work, so they won't know whether I'm lying or not. At least, I hope not. Sweat prickles on the back of my neck. I say, "Omar and I are friends. There's nothing going on."

The reaction is instant. Bark ripples from my fingertips and over my hands. Mom gasps, her hands flying to her mouth. She shrieks, "Vin! His hand! His arms! What's happening?"

Dad's eyebrows are practically in his hairline. He grabs my arm where there's still skin showing, as if he can make the growing stop. But the bark creeps under his hand and bubbles all the way up to my elbow. "Matteo," he says in his fireman-to-the-rescue voice. "What is this?"

I pry his hand from my arm. "I'm okay. I promise." I pick

off a shard of wood. "It's bark. It comes right off. It's like my super-armor—"

"Your poor skin," Mom cries, tears budding in the corners of her eyes. "Your beautiful skin. Oh, baby, I'm so sorry I didn't believe you." She clears her throat, her voice dropping in pitch. "This is terrible. We'll get you help right away."

Dad says, "I'll put a call in to Dr. Wilson immediately."

I step back from them. "Maybe I don't want a doctor." I smile to prove I'm okay. "What if this is just me? I don't understand why or how yet, but it's got something to do with the tree in Creekside Park and the family bat and a whole bunch of other things. Omar and Azura have been helping me figure it all out, and I think we're really close to an answer."

Both of my parents look hurt and confused. Mom's lips tremble. "You told your friends about this? Before us? We're your *parents*."

"I already told you that." My voice cracks. I don't want them to feel bad, but they're not listening to me. "I was nervous about how you'd react, and Azura and Omar believed me. And they—they don't think I'm a freak."

Mom *tsks* me. "We do *not* think you're a freak." But her eyes shift upward when she says that, which pretty much means she's lying. Guess I'm not the only person in the family who has a tell when they're not being honest.

"Matteo, we can help you," Dad says. "Whatever this is, whatever is really going on, we'll find a way to make you better."

Those words hit hardest. All he ever wants me to be is better. I'm never ever enough. My sadness simmers into rage and my words come out red-hot. I shout, "This is exactly what I was afraid of. You think I'm broken. That I need to be *fixed!* Why can't you see me the way Azura and Omar do? When Azura found out, she thought I was magic. And Omar thought I was a superhero. And, lately, I haven't been feeling all that bad about who I am! What if I don't want to be better because I already *am* better?"

Dad looks at me seriously. "Matteo, *this* cannot be good for you." He looks at the bark and doesn't even try to hide his disgust. "If what you're saying is, in fact, what's going on, you can't go through life like this. What'll people think when they see bark instead of skin? People can be cruel, Matteo. I don't want anything getting in the way of you living your life, and I won't always be here to protect you."

I crumple in on myself. "You aren't listening."

"We hear you," Mom says, even though she obviously doesn't. "We do. And we love you so, so much. All we want is what's best for you. This isn't what's best." Her lips curl into a pitying frown.

Another gut punch. "But—"

"We're getting you help," says Dad. "I'll call Dr. Wilson."

His eyes wander to the leafy bat on the floor. "And I don't want you exerting yourself until we know what's really going on. No more baseball until we get to the bottom of this."

"That's not fair," I say. "I'm finally getting good!" I'm so mad, I might cry, but I don't want to give them the satisfaction of seeing me upset. I'm a tornado of feelings. I'm finally *doing* what I've been watching the pros and Tyler and Omar be good at all these years. I'm becoming one of the Lorenzini men! And I don't want to miss out on time with Omar. We just became friends again!

Dad ruffles my hair. "You don't have to worry about that right now. We'll figure this out. You'll be back to normal in no time."

Normal. That word tips me over the edge, and finally, I break. A fat, hot tear rolls down my cheek.

Mom swoops in to wipe it away. Then she pulls back awkwardly, like she's suddenly afraid she'll catch my tree-growing disease, and says, "Why don't you change and, uh, clean up? I'll put on some hot water."

Dad grabs the bat on his way out.

"Where are you taking that?" I ask.

"See if I can fix it," he says. "Otherwise, I'll have to junk it, I guess."

"You can't throw it away. It's special. Isn't it?"

He pauses in the doorway. "Yeah, it was."

CREEKSIDE DOCUMENTARY TRANSCRIPT #24

SUBJECT: JIMMY BRIAR

· ·

JIMMY BRIAR

Saw a baby bird fall out of the tree one time, the one my dad says they're cutting down after the bicentennial celebration.

AZURA GONZALEZ

What happened to the bird? Did you help it?

JIMMY BRIAR

Didn't need to. It wasn't moving its wings, but the little guy just started floating up, like it was light as a feather. Floated right back to its nest.

AZURA GONZALEZ

That's amazing.

JIMMY BRIAR

Mom always tells me that tree takes care of us. Even the littlest bird. I wonder what'll watch over us when it's gone.

TWENTY-FIVE

I think all night about how to convince Mom and Dad that I'm okay. That this whole growing thing is really, truly real and good and not *bad*. That maybe I'm special. I just have to figure out why the heck this is happening to me, and then maybe they'll get that I'm not messed up.

But when I come down Sunday morning with a ring of leaves around my head, Mom nearly faints, and Dad tells me to brush that stuff out of my hair. I pluck the leaves one by one and don't bother to grow the rest of the day.

To make matters worse, by that afternoon, all of Creekside seems to be talking about me. My parents' cell phones buzz constantly. Curious neighbors keep calling to see if I'm "all right," but Mom says they're just "fishing for gossip." Dad refuses to even pick up his phone. "None of their business," he mutters, puttering from one end of the house to the other.

The longer the day goes on, the more they treat me like a porcelain vase. Every word they speak is soft. They move around me like if they touch me, I might topple. I'm not fragile, but the more they treat me like I am, the more afraid I become that I'll shatter.

No, that's not the right word. Explode. *That's* it. I'm going to burst into a million pieces because none of this is right, but no matter what I do or say, they refuse to listen.

It isn't until four in the afternoon, when Azura shows up on my doorstep, that I feel any sort of relief. Her blue hair is frizzy, and she's wearing a wrinkled T-shirt. She looks as frazzled as I feel, but it's good to see someone who isn't looking at me like I'm from Mars.

"How are you?" she asks. She clutches a large paper bag to her chest. Her eyes drift to my hands.

I wave them in front of her. "Fine, I guess. Just dealing with my parents now that they know about me treeing out."

She looks at me pityingly. "How are they handling, uh, *everything?*"

As if in response, Dad walks by, cell phone to his ear, saying, "I've been online all day, but I haven't found anything except maybe a fungal infection or—" He waves to Azura, and then crosses into the other room, back to his conversation. "I just don't know. I've never seen anything like it."

I point in Dad's direction. "It's been going a lot like that."

"I'm sorry. I honestly thought they'd be more support-ive." Her forehead scrunches. "Did he really just say 'fungal infection'?"

I rub my left temple. "Yeah. It's been . . . a lot. Mom's the same way. They're both hoping Dr. Wilson has some miracle medicine that can save me, but she's out of town until tomorrow afternoon."

"Ummmm. That's ridiculous. You're not sick." She hugs the bag tighter to her chest. "I do need to show you some-thing though."

"What is it?" I ask, my mouth watering. "Did you bring cupcakes?"

She shakes her head.

"Muffins?"

She peers over my shoulder, eyeing Dad nervously. "Not here."

"Come on. We can go up to my room."

I'm not supposed to close the bedroom door all the way when I have friends over, so I leave it cracked open just a bit. If Mom or Dad come by, we'll hear the floor creak.

Azura plops to the carpet. She sets the bag in front of her. "Last night I was helping Dad close up the bakery, and something weird happened. He has this rolling pin that's been in the family for generations. My grandma made the *best* bread with it. Like, no joke. When she passed away,

Dad had it mounted on a plaque and hung up in the shop."

I nod, picturing the exact rolling pin in my head. "Yeah. I've seen it hanging on the wall behind the counter. Why does that matter?"

"Because," she says. "Look."

She rolls back the crumpled top of the paper bag. Then she reaches in and pulls out something that could have been a rolling pin once upon a time. But now its handles end in fibrous roots, and the roller is spikey and crusted in bark. It looks just like the family bat after yesterday's game!

"How did that happen?" I ask.

She looks at me. "I was hoping you could tell me."

I frown. "*I* didn't do this."

She doesn't look convinced. "Matteo, it's getting all tree-ish. You've gotta have something to do with it. I know it."

I cross my arms. "Wouldn't I know if I did?"

She tugs at a gangly growth. "Do you know what this is? It's a root. Do you know what happens when I pluck one off? Another grows right back. Matteo, you and this rolling pin are connected. I can feel it."

I don't know if I should be insulted or not. "I'm not the same as a rolling pin." But I wonder if the family bat is. If the rolling pin is still growing, maybe the bat is too. I wonder if Dad will be able to fix it or if I ruined our family heirloom forever. My stomach double knots.

"I know that," she says. "But this was just an old hunk

of wood until yesterday. Whatever is going on with you, it's spreading. I don't think this is just about you anymore."

"But this *is* about me," I say. "Your dad isn't going to start treating you like you're from outer space because your *rolling pin* is acting funky."

"That's not what I'm saying," she huffs. "What if this rolling pin is part of the answer? Just like the letters in the tree. Oh! That reminds me: I did some digging on Lisa Lemon."

I lean in a little closer. Finally something I actually want to hear. "What did you find?"

She pulls out her phone and scrolls to her notes app. "She grew up in town and used to work for the *Creekside Herald*, so I was able to find a lot of articles she wrote. Mostly about happenings in town, but she also had a column all about gardening and, get this—*trees*. She was a total conservationist."

"Whoa," I say. "So you think she has—*had*—something to do with the tree magic?" I pause. "But what's her connection to Mr. Kowalski?"

"I'm still working on the whole tree-magic thing," Azura says. "But the Mr. Kowalski bit . . . well, Lisa Lemon married a guy named Clarence Lemon when she was twenty. My guess is she and Mr. Kowalski were in love, something happened, and then she married someone else. Maybe he knows a secret about her that she never told anyone else! Maybe that's why the tree sent us to him. Since she isn't around, *he* can give us the answers!"

My brain hurts. "But what does all of that have to do with me? Why would the tree want us to find her? Or talk to Mr. Kowalski?"

Azura purses her lips. "Look, I'm still working on the details, but we're a few steps closer than we were, okay?"

"Yeah," I say. "Thanks for doing all that. I just need answers soon, or I'm afraid my parents will lock me away forever."

"Don't be so dramatic. You know they'd never do that."

I stand up. "I don't know what they'll do!"

She shoves the rolling pin back in the bag. "Why don't we take your mind off it for a while?" She swipes to a different app on her phone, a playful grin on her face. "I got a few new interviews yesterday for our Creekside documentary. One of them is someone you *might* like to hear from."

The documentary is so not what I care about right now, but I say, "Who?"

There's a gleam in her eye. "Omar."

Okay, so maybe I am interested. "You interviewed him? Without me?"

"He was worried about you, so I was trying to distract him," she says. "Did you know his great-aunt ran the first post office in town? He actually had a lot of interesting stories about her and Creekside."

The question comes out of my mouth before I can stop myself. "Did he say anything about me?"

She laughs. "We were talking about the town! Why would he say anything about you?"

I fidget with the cuff of my sock. "You're right."

She shoves my shoulder. "I'm just kidding. He *may* have said something about you. But you've got to watch first. I want to know what you think."

I groan, making space for her on the bed. "Fine. You win." She hops up next to me and we watch the small screen in her hand. Omar's face, neck, and shoulders fill the rectangle. He's wearing his Blue Whales baseball jersey. Seeing him makes me feel like a shaken can of soda. I don't take my eyes off the interview for the full seven minutes and thirty-eight seconds.

It ends without a single mention of me. I glare at her. "He didn't say anything about me!"

"Not on *camera*," she says.

I squint. "That's cheating. What did he say?"

"He asked if I'd talked to you since the game. He wanted to know if you were okay."

"Why didn't he get ahold of me himself?"

Azura shrugs. "Don't ask me. I have no idea how boys' brains work. But he did say you crushed it at the game. Well, until you ran away."

I flush. "He did?"

"He did." Now she's grinning from ear to ear. "Something about a killer catch."

"For real?"

"I'm not saying it again," she deadpans. But then her face cracks into another smile. "Matteo, even if your parents don't get it yet, Omar and I, we think you're awesome. Just the way you are. It's okay for you to think you are too even if they don't . . . yet."

"Thanks." My muscles unclench. I eye the bag with the rolling pin. If things are getting weirder, we really do need answers, and soon. "Tomorrow we should try talking to Mr. Kowalski again. First thing in the morning?"

"Let's do it." Azura hops off the bed. "I should get home." She picks the bag off the floor. "I'll see you tomorrow, okay?"

I follow her downstairs. "Thanks for coming over."

She hugs me. "What are friends for?"

But when she's gone, and the sounds of Mom on the phone and Dad clacking away at his laptop come back, it dawns on me that maybe Azura is more than a friend—that she's family. My family. The family I need when my parents feel so very far away.

CREEKSIDE DOCUMENTARY TRANSCRIPT #25

SUBJECT: OMAR JONES

. . . .

AZURA GONZALEZ

What's your favorite thing about living here?

OMAR JONES

Aside from Mrs. Curtis's ice cream at Conehead's—rocky road for life—I'd say my favorite thing is my friends.

AZURA GONZALEZ

Okay, but your friends aren't the town. What do you like most about Creekside?

OMAR JONES

I think you're wrong. My favorite people are what make this my favorite place. Well, them and rocky road ice cream.

TWENTY-SIX

It takes a lot of convincing, but by Sunday night Mom and Dad *finally* agree to let me go to school the next morning. Even as I'm walking out the door to meet Azura, Mom asks, "Are you sure you're okay? We have your appointment with Dr. Wilson after school. You can always wait until tomorrow. I don't mind calling you in sick."

I'm not sick, I think, but I say, "I'm fine. I promise." I squeeze her tight and then shut the door behind me. I've answered that question at least forty-seven times in the past twenty-four hours. My response hasn't changed. I wish they could see I'm okay, that I'm *more* than okay, but it's like whenever they talk to me, they're looking right through me.

But when Azura and I walk into school, whispers come from every direction. Even the seventh and eighth graders are suddenly paying attention to me. One girl points her phone at us and I'm sure she takes my picture. Azura swats at her, telling her to delete whatever she took. The girl denies she did anything, but Azura stands in her way until she shows us her photos. Fortunately, there aren't any pictures or recordings of me.

Hard as it is not to let all the attention get to me, I try my best to focus on our mission: talk to Mr. Kowalski. For real this time.

Omar is standing outside the library when we arrive. He's wearing a red Nike T-shirt and jeans. A single earbud dangles from his right ear. I was a little nervous he'd ditch me after what happened at the game, even with Azura's reassurances, but he high-fives me like nothing's changed. "Azura told me we've got some investigating to do. How're you feeling? I was worried about you after the game, but I didn't want to bug you. Figured you had enough going on at home."

"You wouldn't bug me," I say. "I'm okay, but my parents were all over me this weekend. Mom's acting like she must have hallucinated the bat growing, and Dad's latest diagnosis is that I have a hormone imbalance."

"Hold up." Omar makes a weird face like he's trying not to laugh. "Hormones? He's blaming . . . *puberty?*"

I can't help cracking a smile. "Pretty much."

"Shoot." Omar chuckles. "And you just thought you'd be getting some chest hair!"

"Gross," says Azura, breaking up our laughter. She

glances up at the clock. "We've only got a few minutes before first period. Come on."

Still laughing, we follow her into the dim library. Mr. Kowalski sits at the circulation desk, his glasses perched on the tip of his nose. Light from the computer screen casts long shadows over his face. He does a double take when he sees us.

"Kids," he says, clearing his throat. "Good morning."

We approach the desk, all three of us resting our arms on the countertop.

"Azura and I wanted to apologize for last week," I start off. "If we offended you by asking about LL."

Mr. Kowalski's face is unreadable, but he removes his glasses. "No, I wasn't offended. More . . . surprised. I—I haven't talked about that person in a very long time."

Azura looks at me knowingly and then leans in. "So LL *is* somebody?"

The old man nods. "A dear friend. Someone I loved very much."

I glance at Azura—she was right. I whisper, "So you *were* in love with Lisa Lemon?"

"What happened to her?" Azura asks eagerly. "We need to know everything."

Mr. Kowalski's face scrunches, not like he's upset but like he's confused. "Lisa Lemon? Haven't heard that name in a million years." A cheeky grin spreads across his lips. "Is *that* who you thought those initials were referring to?"

"Uh." Azura looks at me. I look back at her. "Yes?"

Omar's hands fly up. "Look, I'm only catching up here, but if we're not talking about this Lisa Lemon person, who *are* we talking about?"

"Well, for starters, we're not talking about a 'she.'" Mr. Kowalski lays his palms flat on the desk. "LL's a he."

Azura's mouth forms a perfect circle. "Ohhhhh."

But I'm still processing. Omar suddenly feels very close to me. My hands get all clammy. I almost can't believe what I'm about to say. "You were in love with . . . a guy?"

Mr. Kowalski nods. "That's correct."

"So if LL isn't Lisa Lemon," says Azura, "who was he? The real LL."

Mr. Kowalski's eyes flash at me. Then they fall to his hands, and he stares at them for a very long time. After what feels like forever, he says very quietly, "Matteo, I don't think I should be saying this, to you of all people."

Now I'm getting anxious. "Why not?"

His eyes shift to the ceiling, like he's looking for answers up there. "Oh Lord. It's been long enough, I suppose." Then Mr. Kowalski exhales heavily and says, "LL is Ludo Lorenzini—your grandfather, Matteo." Azura's and Omar's heads whip to me. Quiet hangs in the air. My heartbeat thrums in my ears. Then Mr. Kowalski goes on, talking a little faster, a little louder. "We grew up together. We were best friends, and as we got older, well, we became more than friends."

I can't believe it. Did Mr. Kowalski really just say he was in love with MY GRANDPA?

I literally have no words.

But Azura doesn't miss a beat. "What happened to him?"

"Times were different back then," Mr. Kowalski says. He pauses, looking at the door. Then he rubs his eyes, which have misted over. "I'm sorry. I shouldn't be—I've never shared this with students before. Never thought I'd have to. Kids haven't shown much interest in me the past few years. I'm just the old librarian, you know?"

"We don't think that," I say, still fighting off the shock. "Tell us. Please."

Mr. Kowalski's nose scrunches like he might cry. "What I'm going to say, please keep it between us, okay?"

I look to Azura, and she nods sharply as if to say *of course*. But I'm nervous to look at Omar. I'm not sure what he thinks about all this guys-liking-guys stuff. Part of me wants to know, but part of me doesn't. What if he says something homophobic? He wouldn't, would he? I'm anxious, but Mr. Kowalski's waiting, and we're so close to getting answers. Hesitantly, I turn to him.

Omar immediately nods, confident and serious. Relief

washes over me. Maybe gay things don't bother him. Maybe he's even okay with gay people. My heart hiccups. *Maybe he's even* . . . No, I can't let myself go there right now. *This isn't about you and your crush, Matteo.* I shake off my thought spiral. Then, confident in my answer, I say, "We know how to keep secrets."

Mr. Kowalski goes on, still a little shaky, "I appreciate that. Well, I've been comfortable saying I'm gay for some time now, but back when I was with Ludo, it wasn't easy. We couldn't be together." He chuckles darkly. "Well, we *could*, but that came with complications. I would have lost my family. My credibility. My future. Ludo would have lost all those things too."

"That must have been hard," Omar says.

"An understatement if there ever was one," Mr. Kowalski agrees.

My heart hurts. I have so many questions, but I start with, "So if you guys were secret boyfriends, why did you carve 'For LL' into the tree? Wouldn't that make your relationship kind of obvious?"

Mr. Kowalski sniffs. "We'd watched other couples carve their initials into the tree all throughout junior high and high school, but we knew we never could. By the time graduation rolled around, Ludo decided he was done hiding. He wanted to be the man he was expected to be—to have a wife and children. He thought it would be easier. I was

192

heartbroken, but I understood. At least, I thought I did. It was all just so different back then. That carving was my parting gift to him. My way of letting go and saying good-bye."

"So he married Matteo's grandma?" Omar asks.

Mr. Kowalski sniffs. "He did."

"But he didn't love her," Azura says.

"Oh, in his way, I think he did. For a time." Mr. Kowalski looks at me. "But he especially loved your father, Matteo."

There's so much Dad hasn't told me. I'm all questions. *Is Mr. Kowalski the reason my grandparents got divorced? Did Grandpa leave Creekside because he was gay?* A twist of nausea rises in my throat. *Is that why Dad won't talk about Grandpa? Because he knows he's gay?* But before I can ask any of my dozens of questions, Omar shifts on his feet next to me and says, "When did you come out?"

I keep noting his reactions to all of this. He seems calm yet interested, which makes me wonder if maybe, just *maybe*, the idea of me liking him and him liking me *back* isn't impossible.

"Much later in life, to my friends," says Mr. Kowalski. "The world changed. Things seemed to get better for people like me. I wasn't ashamed anymore, and I wasn't as scared."

There are so many things I need to know, but I can't go to Dad for answers. If I don't ask Mr. Kowalski now, I might miss my one chance to learn more about my family and why Dad never talks about Grandpa. This might even be my chance to help Dad, instead of him always trying to help me. "My grandpa," I say. "What happened to him? Dad won't tell me anything. I know he and my grandma got divorced and then he disappeared. But Dad's hardly ever said anything else about him." I frown. "Wait. If my grandparents got divorced because Grandpa's gay, then why isn't he with *you*?"

Mr. Kowalski's mouth opens, then closes, and opens again. Maybe I got too personal in my questions. But then he says, "Your grandpa left Creekside because, well—" He scratches his right eyebrow with the back of his thumb. "I think—I think it was all too much for him. He was ashamed. Sad. Even with the divorce, he struggled to call himself gay. As much as your grandpa loved your dad and this town, accepting the truth scared him more than anything. So he left. His absence hit all of us hard. And not just me and your father—the whole town. The Lorenzinis have been here since Creekside was founded two hundred years ago. He was an essential part of town. Volunteering at church, mowing so-and-so's yard because they'd broken a leg—you could always count on him."

Mr. Kowalski laughs lightly to himself. "I used to say he was as reliable as the oak tree in Creekside Park—steadfast, dependable, and not going anywhere." He sighs. "That's probably why it hurt so much when he suddenly wasn't around." Mr. Kowalski looks directly at me. "That tree. He always said it was important to your family. That's why I knew it would be especially meaningful for him to finally have his initials carved on it from someone he truly loved and who loved him back."

The tree. More puzzle pieces are coming together. Here's one more reason to believe that it's connected to my family. Somehow Grandpa is part of the answer to what's going on with me. I just know it. But how?

"You never tried to reach out to him?" Azura asks.

Mr. Kowalski shakes his head. "I couldn't bring myself to, but he wrote me a letter once. I was so angry then, so hurt. I threw it away after I read it. If I'm remembering correctly, he mentioned writing to your father too, Matteo. Said he told Vinny the truth about everything. The divorce, why he left, even me." He rubs the wrinkles under his eyes. "But I'm sure your dad never mentioned that."

"No," I say. "He didn't." It's hitting me just how little I know not just about Grandpa but about Dad. He must really be hurt and ashamed to keep so much from me. What does that mean for me? Mom's question about what's going on between me and Omar felt very wink-wink, which makes me think she knows how I feel about him, but what about Dad? Does he know? Will he still love me if I come out? (Or if I can't stop turning into a tree?) I'm getting sick to my stomach. Will he ignore me? Kick me out? What if he wants to "fix" every single part of me?

"You could still try to find him, couldn't you?" says Omar, bringing my attention back to the conversation. "What if he's waiting for you?"

Mr. Kowalski chuckles. "I appreciate your optimism, but some things are just not meant to be. Besides, I wouldn't even know how to go about finding Ludo. We lost touch so long ago."

"But that's not right. It's not fair," I say. "None of this is."

Brrring! The warning bell rings.

"I'm so sorry, Matteo. We can talk more about this later. Maybe I shouldn't have said anything. I hope I didn't share too much." He clears his throat. "I'm afraid I did. I'm so sorry."

Azura touches my arm. "We'd better go."

But I can't move. Sure, we're getting answers, but all of this is too big. Way more than I bargained for. Thinking about Mr. Kowalski, my grandpa, Dad. My heart fragments in a million pieces, each one lodging like a splinter in my chest. The sharp pain makes it hard to breathe. I'm so angry and sad for Mr. Kowalski and Grandpa, for Dad, for me. Frustration burns under my skin. My fists squeeze tight at my sides. *Why is this on me to fix? Why do I have to figure this out? I'm just a kid!*

A queasy feeling makes my knees buckle. There's another emotion hiding behind my anger—guilt. But this *can't* be my fault, even though somehow it feels like *I'm* responsible. I don't want to be, but deep down, I know I need to help Mr. Kowalski and my grandpa. I have to fix my family. If I can find Grandpa and talk to him, then I can fix everything. But I don't even know where to start! I want to scream. *Why does all of this have to be so hard?*

Suddenly, my head hurts so bad, I *do* scream. My eyes squeeze shut. I press my hands to the sides of my head, pushing against the pain. I scream and scream until I run out of air. The pain lessens. My eyes flutter open.

Omar's hand is on my shoulder. "Are you okay?"

The lights in the library flicker before I can respond. Azura whispers nervously, her eyes on the wall behind me. "Uh, Matteo."

"What?" I say, my voice scratchy. The lights flicker again.

Mr. Kowalski stands, replacing his glasses on his nose. "What in the world?"

Omar, Azura, and I turn. Paint chips fall from the walls all around us. Fissures open like the surface of a frozen lake in spring. From the cracks and crevices emerge calluses of bark, dark brown and craggy. *Oh no. Oh no, no, no! What did I do?* The room quakes. Overhead, the ceiling splits and a bough breaks through, raining twigs and flecks of bark in my hair.

"Get out, get out!" Mr. Kowalski says, shooing us out of the library with his cane.

But I can't move. I look down. My feet are stuck. Serpentine roots shoot through the soles and sides of my shoes. Panic fills my lungs. Whatever's happening now, this is new. This doesn't feel like what usually happens to me at all. Something is very wrong. More of my roots rupture the floor. I'm destroying the library. I've lost control and put us all in danger!

"Matteo, let's go!" Azura shouts, holding the library door open for Mr. Kowalski to shuffle-run through. Omar isn't far behind.

"I'm stuck," I shout back. "My feet are growing!"

The ceiling shudders above the circulation desk. Another branch crashes into the room. I throw my arms over my head to protect myself from tumbling debris.

Then there are more arms under my shoulders, hugging my chest, pulling me backward. My head spins. It's Omar. He's come back for me.

"Use your legs," he shouts in my ear. "PUSH!"

I twist my feet, shoving against the ground. "I'm trying!"

"It's coming down," he says. "We've got to go now!"

Anger and frustration flare inside me. "Why is this *happening?*" I yank hard, and my left foot unlatches from the floor. My shoe's in tatters.

"That's it," Omar says. "Now the other one." He pulls harder, squeezing so tight it hurts.

I groan, and with a wrenching *creee-AAK*, I free my right foot. We topple to the ground. My feet are almost completely naked, my shoes and socks destroyed by the roots and twigs and bark caking my skin. All the bits of tree barnacled to my feet make it difficult to stand. Omar helps me up as light bulbs shatter, and we sprint out of the library.

CREEKSIDE DOCUMENTARY TRANSCRIPT #26

SUBJECT: ALICIA JETT

. . . .

ALICIA JETT

I always thought the tree was kind of creepy. I know some people like that they can see it wherever they're at in town, but me? I feel like I'm always being watched.

AZURA GONZALEZ

But don't you feel like it's a guardian angel?

ALICIA JETT

I don't believe in angels.

AZURA GONZALEZ

What do you believe in?

ALICIA JETT

Science. And ghosts. Yeah, I believe in science and ghosts.

AZURA GONZALEZ

Well, okay then.

TWENTY-SEVEN

Thanks to me, school shuts down before first period even begins. But only me, Azura, and Omar know why. Poor Mr. Kowalski is so discombobulated that he keeps telling everyone there was an earthquake, even though I'm sure he's got to know walls don't grow branches during any known natural disaster.

Now all us kids are standing outside, waiting for someone to pick us up. Alarms blare in the building. Azura, Omar, and I hang out as far away from the noise as possible. My bare feet are still a mess of bark and twigs. Azura and Omar shield me from view while I sit and pick at my skin. I don't want any questions; I'm too full of my own after talking with Mr. Kowalski.

Teachers march around with grim expressions, mouths pressed to walkie-talkies. Some hold clipboards, marking off students they see and yelling the names of those they don't. No one's hurt, but a police car, an ambulance, and a fire truck show up regardless.

My stomach clenches. Just what I need: for Dad to hop out of the engine. But he doesn't. He must be doing something else. Or is he off today? I can't remember. I'm just glad that, for once, I'm in luck.

I watch the other kids while the first responders infiltrate our school. Some kids look worried and some stare at me, whispering and pointing, but most are quiet, watching the far-left library window on the first floor, where a branch the width of a garbage can shoots through.

"That was close," Omar whispers.

Azura leans toward me. "What happened in there?"

I can't help interpreting her question as, *What's wrong with you? How could you let that happen? You almost killed us!*

"I—I don't know," I say. "I was upset, and then I felt sick, and my head hurt and—" I look her in the eye. I need her to believe me. "It was an accident. I wasn't trying to hurt anyone."

"I didn't mean it like that," she says. "We just haven't seen anything like *that* happen before."

Shadows approaches us. "Hey."

Tyler and Freddie stand shoulder to shoulder. They look plain mean. I crisscross my legs to hide my feet.

Azura steps in front of me. "What do you want?"

"Look, no one's gonna say it," says Tyler, "but we're not

totally clueless. We know what's going on. This freak"—he points at me—"turns his bat into a whacked-out bush at the game, and now the library is wrecked because a tree decided to bust it up from the inside out." He dodges Azura and needles his finger into my forehead. "I *saw* you run out of the library. This is your fault."

Freddie nods in agreement, crossing his arms over his chest.

I shove Tyler's finger away. "You don't know what you're talking about."

"Oh yeah?" He dips down farther into my space. His trademark Cheeto breath clouds around me. "Prove you didn't do it, freak. Prove you didn't just try to kill us all."

"Yeah, prove it," Freddie echoes.

"Leave him alone," says Omar, failing to wedge himself between me and Tyler.

Panic vibrates in my chest. I can't stay here. I try to stand, but Tyler keeps coming at me, shoving his finger into my shirt. "What are you gonna do? Huh?"

Azura leaves, saying she's going to get a teacher, but Tyler ignores her. He pushes me again, so hard that I fall backward. But I roll up quick and push myself to standing. That flutter of worry inside me transforms into annoyance and anger. It becomes rage. A fiery cool sensation flashes through my body, past my knees, through my feet. I worm my bare toes into the earth.

Tyler comes at me again but this time he face-plants into the grass. Freddie freezes. So does Omar. Their eyes linger on Tyler's feet, which are tied up in leafy, twinning roots. Even I'm a little surprised. I didn't have to lie to grow. Something's definitely changed—I'm just not sure what.

Tyler pushes himself up, his face glowing with realization. "*That* was you too. The other day at the cemetery. You were the one trying to freak us out!" He turns bloodred. "I'm gonna destroy you."

I don't give it another thought. I run, fast as I can, away from the school. Omar shouts after me, but I've got to get away from this mess.

Only, my mess follows me. As I run through downtown Creekside, wind gusting in my ears, the whole world turns upside down. With each step I take, more of the town trees out, and none of it makes any sense. I'm not lying, and I'm definitely not *trying* to grow or make anything tree-ish happen. But there's a wooden ladder climbing out of the third-story fire station window. The two stubby legs below the bottom rung scale the brick face of the building. Then there's the wooden café sign for Creekside Coffee & Tea swinging wildly back and forth like an invisible hand is paddling it. An upturned wooden bowl waddles past on spindly roots, miniature bowls toddling after it like duck-lings, completely stopping me in my tracks. Those roots remind me of how Azura's rolling pin grew. The oak's magic is spreading farther and farther, and I can't control it. My bare feet, still covered in bits of bark, scratch the cement. All these things—it all comes back to the tree and me. But how? Why *me*?

I try to shake what I'm seeing from my mind. None of this can really be happening. I'm dreaming. I've got to be. This is all too much. I start running again, but I'm cut off by a broom handle bouncing down the sidewalk like a pogo stick. A shop clerk from the local grocery nearly knocks me over as he chases after it.

"What is going on?" I shout. A stray leaf whips into my face. An *oak* leaf. Of course. I brush it aside, but now I know where I'm running to—the one thing that's at the center of all this.

Creekside Park is nearly empty when I dash through the entryway. I march right up to the oak, glaring at the branches. I'm out of breath and fuming. The dark, oozing vein along the trunk is thicker and bolder than before. It's getting worse. There's no doubt in my mind: it's dying, and somehow, it's taking me and the town down with it.

"What do you want from me?" I shout. "You're messing up everything! Tell me what I need to do to make this stop!"

Wind ruffles the new leaves. A squirrel chitters somewhere in the upper branches.

"Is that all you're going to do?" I shout. "You can make my body do weird things and destroy a library, but you can't tell me what I need to know? Why *me*? What am I supposed to do? You really expect me to find my grandpa? Dad won't even talk about him! No one knows how to find him! And even if I do, what am I supposed to say? 'Hi, I'm your freak grandson. My world is falling apart, and I need your help so please come home?'" The tree doesn't react. My fury grows. "DO SOMETHING."

I circle the trunk, getting angrier by the second. Cricket's little tree is still there, an inch taller than before. I wish I'd never buried him here. He deserves better than this. I scour the bark, hoping to see some leaves in the shape of a word telling me what to do next, but the tree doesn't budge.

"You know they're going to cut you down in a few weeks, right?" I shout. "You're sick. You deserve to get cut down. When they do, I hope everyone forgets you ever existed!"

The tree stands quiet. No wind passes. No birds chirp; no squirrels dart through the boughs. I wait in the silence, but nothing happens. "Please. Help me."

I wait a minute more, but the tree doesn't grow or shake or bend. Then I trudge home, defeated and hopeless.

SUBJECT: JEREMY KOSTA

. . . .

JEREMY KOSTA

Trees are dangerous. My cat got stuck in a tree once.

MATTEO LORENZINI

Okay, but is that the tree's fault?

JEREMY KOSTA

I didn't say it was.

MATTEO LORENZINI

Trees aren't dangerous. Your cat just wasn't using its brain.

JEREMY KOSTA

Uh, I thought this was supposed to be a documentary about Creekside?

MATTEO LORENZINI

Yeah. Whatever. What do you want to say?

TWENTY-EIGHT

"I don't normally make house calls, but . . ." Dr. Wilson trails off, her mouth hidden behind an aquamarine surgical mask. Her eyes linger on the knobs and twigs piled on the countertop that I broke off after I got home from the park. Dad insisted I keep them as evidence.

"But what?" I say. I'm wearing a mask too. Doctor's orders.

She shakes her head and takes my feet in her gloved hands. I picked off all the bark so they're back to smooth skin. She drags her thumb over the soft pad of my foot. I wince. "Does that hurt?" she asks.

"No. Tickles."

She harumphs and flips my foot up to examine the heel. Then she sits back and turns to Mom and Dad, who've been standing near the stove, waiting.

"Well?" Mom asks.

Dr. Wilson sighs. "I hate to say it, but far as I can tell,

there's nothing wrong with him. His temperature, blood pressure, pulse, breathing . . ." She looks at me. "You're perfectly healthy."

I exhale a sigh I've been holding all day. At least I was wrong about one thing: even if the tree is dying, I'm not. Dr. Wilson saying I'm healthy is exactly what I needed to hear.

"But he's not," Dad says. "There's clearly something wrong. Can't you run some more tests?"

I stare at the floor. Of course he doesn't believe her. He doesn't believe me either.

"I've taken blood samples, but obviously I can't process those here."

Mom chimes in. "It could be too much iron or potassium or something. Too much of a good thing, right? I've been reading more about—"

My fingernails bite into my palms. "Dr. Wilson said I'm fine. Why does there *have* to be something wrong with me? Do you want there to be?"

My parents' faces turn gray. "Don't be ridiculous," Dad says.

Mom comes around the counter. "We want to help you."

"Doesn't seem like it," I mumble.

Dr. Wilson packs her bag in the awkward silence that follows. She takes off her gloves, tossing them in the trash. "Well," she says, clearing her throat, "at the very least, we know that we don't, in fact, know what is going on with you,

Matteo. For now, considering the, um, *oddities* happening around town and for the safety of yourself and others, I recommend you quarantine until we have more information."

My heart sinks. "Quarantine?"

"Do you really think that's necessary?" Mom asks.

Dr. Wilson doesn't remove her mask as she packs up. "I'm afraid so. But once we know more, Matteo can return to life as usual. I'll follow up as soon as the blood tests come back." Her bag snaps shut. "If anything should arise, please don't hesitate to call. Here's my personal number, just in case." She hands Mom a slip of paper, a phone number scrawled on it in blue ink.

"Thank you," Mom says, taking it from her. "We appreciate you coming all the way here."

I fume. Now I'm not just a freak but a prisoner too. Everything keeps getting worse.

Dad breaks the silence after Dr. Wilson leaves. "Can we do anything for you?"

I can't believe the question. "*Do* anything for me?" I spit back. "What about believe me? Or tell me I'll be okay?" I almost mention Grandpa, but I can't even go there right now. Since I got home from the park, all they've done is smother me with questions and reprimand me for not waiting at school for one of them to pick me up.

"Of course you're okay, honey," Mom says. "But this is for the best. Just a precaution."

I shake my head. "What if 'for the best' isn't for *my* best?"

"Sport, we'll get this sorted out," Dad says. "You'll see."

I don't want to hear any more of this. "Whatever." I stomp upstairs and slam my bedroom door, leaving the sound of my parents' muffled arguing behind me.

So many thoughts are pinballing around my mind that it's impossible to sleep. I toss and turn so much my sheets wrap completely around my body. I wish I had someone to talk to. Mom and Dad *say* they want to listen and that they care, but they only hear me if I say what they want me to say: That I'm not well. That I need help. That they know what's best.

But they don't.

If they won't listen to what is really going on, then they don't need to hear anything at all.

I'm finally drifting off when something flumps to the floor across my bedroom. I flip over, the sheets boa-constricting tighter around me, and peer through one eye. Shadows and purple-blue light line the floor from my blinds. Nothing seems to have fallen. And the pile of dirty clothes is just like I left it. Maybe I dreamed the noise?

I roll over, frustrated that I have to go back through the process of not thinking enough to fall asleep all over again.

Then a voice whispers, "Matteo."

I sit upright like someone dumped ice water down the back of my shirt. "Who's there?"

My pulse quickens. The room is silent. I reach for the switch on the lamp. My fingers fumble with the knob. Something like firefly glow catches in my peripheral vision and I stop. "Is someone there?" I whisper. I give up on the lamp, following the strange glow. The light bobs near the floor at the foot of my bed.

"Hello?"

Silence.

I must have heard wrong. No one said my name. But what's that weird light?

Slowly, I wriggle out of the sheets and peek over the edge of the bed. A greenish-yellowish orb zooms at my face.

"AHH!"

The orb shouts back, "AHH, YOURSELF!"

I crab crawl backward. "What are you?"

"What are *you?*" the thing replies, mocking my high pitch. "Is that how you greet an old friend?" The ball of light swishes toward me.

It can't be. I rub my eyes once, then a second time. The glowing *whateveritis* is still hovering in front of me. I can't believe what I'm seeing. "Cricket?"

"The one and only!" he says.

The translucent, glowing fish floats at my eye level. He's totally see-through, but I can also make out each individual scale, the slight flutter of his gills opening and closing. His lips pucker. His eyes dart to the left, then the right, taking in the room.

"You can talk? And you're alive?" I shake my head. "But you're *dead*. I buried you—"

"Wait, wait, wait," Cricket says. "I'm DEAD?"

Blood drains from my face. I still feel guilty about what happened to him. "It was an accident. I didn't mean to! I—"

Cricket laughs, looping in a midair circle. "Just kidding. I know I'm dead. You know, being a ghost isn't half-bad. As you noticed, I can talk. And I don't have to stay in that fishbowl. *So* limiting. Now I can swim wherever I want! Ahhh, it's the afterlife for me, kid."

"But . . . how?" I ask. "I don't understand."

"You said it yourself." He swims under the lampshade. The lightbulb flickers, and when he reappears, the light is on. "You buried me. Under the oak tree? *You* did this."

There it is again. That freaking tree. It's like it's haunting me. *Literally.*

"It wasn't *me*," I say. "The *tree* must have turned you into a ghost."

"You, the tree, whatever the case, I'm here!"

"Why, though?" My fingers dig into my hair. "Why is everything going insane? Nothing makes sense."

"You know," Cricket says, "I don't *really* know, but I had this feeling that I was needed. So I popped out of the ground

213

and came here. I didn't make a very good conversationalist in life, so this might actually be an improvement. A voice can be a very useful thing."

"I've got to be dreaming."

"You're NO-ot," Cricket singsongs. He disappears into the pile of clothes on the floor. "Why do you have so many socks?"

I climb out of bed. "What am I supposed to do with a ghostfish?"

Cricket's tail appears in the end of a shirtsleeve. It swishes out, and his bulging eyes burst through a yellowish sock nearby. "Is it just me, or do you have exceptionally smelly feet?"

"Cricket, focus."

The fish darts to my nose. "I'm the essence of focus. Literally the most focused I've been my entire life—okay, not *life* per se—and I want to know about your socks. Can you make fin socks? I would have enjoyed those back in the day. Fish don't tell you this, but that water can get *pretty* chilly."

"I give up." I flump backward and cross my legs. "This is just what I need. Another weird thing I'll have to explain to Mom and Dad."

Cricket flips upside down. "Who says you have to tell them?"

"They find out everything anyway. It's only a matter of time. Then I'll be in quarantine forever."

Cricket backstrokes, musing. "Interesting. *Very* interesting. Tell me more about that."

"You don't actually care."

He flips upright and dashes through the air. His fins squish the sides of my nose. "Oh, but I do! I care. I really do. I care a lot. Please tell me, please!"

I swat him away. "Your fins are cold."

"Like I said," says Cricket. "I need socks."

I crack a grin. "Were you always this full of thoughts when you were alive?"

"You ain't heard the half of it, kid!" He swishes away to my bed and pats the blanket with a fin. "Now, why don't you get over here and tell old Cricket what's been going on? I've missed so much!"

Less reluctant than I'd been feeling a moment ago, I hop back into bed. I sit with my knees against my chest, tug the blanket up, and tuck it around my waist. Cricket floats on top of my knees, his almost-indistinct chin resting in his fins.

The words come slowly at first, but then they flow easily. In no time, it's like when Cricket used to flit around the bowl and I'd tell him about my day. But now I have so many more things to say. About my body and feelings, about Azura and Omar, about Mom and Dad and the baseball team, about Tyler, and Mr. Kowalski and Grandpa, about the documentary and Dr. Wilson, about Creekside and the tree in the park. Cricket listens the whole time, nodding or frowning, and he doesn't interrupt except to say, "Tell me more about that." And the longer I talk, the brighter he seems to glow. After a while, though, I realize it's not the fish that's brightening; it's the whole room. I've talked the night away, and in the new dawn, I find that, tired as I am, I feel a little bit better.

CREEKSIDE DOCUMENTARY TRANSCRIPT #28

SUBJECT: EDWINA WORST

. . . .

MATTEO LORENZINI
What would you like to say? About Creekside?

EDWINA WORST
I love it here. A lot.

MATTEO LORENZINI
Why is that?

EDWINA WORST
*When my parents got divorced, my mom and I moved here.
It's nothing like where we used to live. I feel safe here.*

AZURA GONZALEZ
*I feel safe here too. After my mom passed away, Creekside
took care of me and my dad. I get it. This place—it's special.*

EDWINA WORST
Yeah. It is.

TWENTY-NINE

There's a knock at the front door early Tuesday morning. I'm not supposed to leave my room, but I sneak to the top of the stairs with Cricket on my shoulder and listen.

"Sorry to barge in on you like this so early, Vin, but I've got to follow up on some leads regarding the irregularities going on around town."

"Who's that?" Cricket whispers in my ear.

I know that voice. "Officer James," I whisper back. "The police."

"The police! Whatever they say, it wasn't me!"

I shush him. "They'll hear us."

"We don't know anything about that, Ian," says Dad. "Sorry we can't be of help."

The sound of the front door closing stops. "It's about Matteo," Officer James goes on. "Folks are saying he's connected to the problems. You know Miles Sudbury? His kid

218

Tyler says Matteo had an incident at their baseball game this past weekend. That he can, uh, *make things grow?*" Officer James chuckles to himself. "Look, I know how this sounds, but I just want to ask Matteo a few questions."

Dad's voice is firm. "Now's not a good time, Ian. Matteo's not feeling well."

"Is that so?"

I want to shout down the stairs that it's not true. I feel fine, but I also don't want to talk to Officer James.

"Maybe another time," Dad says. Again, the front door starts to close.

The creak stops. "I don't think you understand, Vin. The town is in a bad way. I'm not one to buy into the super-natural, but all this bark and leaf growing going around town—makes me think about all those folk tales about that oak in Creekside Park. Ridiculous, I know, but I can't help but wonder if maybe there's something to it all. Maybe its disease is spreading. Ask me, that tree should have come down years ago."

"Ian, I respect you, I do," Dad says, "but you can't be serious. A *tree*, responsible for all this? And you think my son's involved? Come on. Matteo's a *kid*. An unwell kid at that. Don't come to my house with your wild accusations and expect me to be on your side. Goodbye."

The door closes on Officer James.

I feel a mixture of relief and resentment. Dad stood up for me, but he called me "unwell." That *word*. It's worse than calling me sick. Like he's afraid I'll never be well.

"Come on," I whisper to Cricket. "We've got our own investigating to do."

Last night, Cricket and I decided the tree sent him to me for a reason: to help me find grandpa. Since the Kaz clue helped us figure out what *LL* stands for, trying to get in touch with Grandpa is the only next step that makes sense. *How* is the only mystery. Mr. Kowalski mentioned that Grandpa sent Dad a letter a long time ago, so it's *possible* Dad kept it, even though Mr. Kowalski threw his out. Mom and Dad are busy downstairs, so it's the perfect time for us to snoop around.

We tiptoe down the hallway and into my parents' bedroom. If Dad's hiding anything, it'll be here. Their king-size bed takes up most of the space. Opposite the window is a long dresser and a standing wardrobe. The first thing I notice catches me by surprise. Leaning against the wardrobe is my bat—*Grandpa's* bat, still covered in twigs and leaves.

"He kept it." I almost reach for it but stop myself. I don't need anything tree-ish happening in the middle of our detective work.

Cricket dives into the dresser, vanishing into the wooden drawers. "Stay focused, Matteo. We've got lots of ground to cover."

"Right," I say, slowly pulling the wardrobe doors open.

Dad's clothes hang neatly in order of formality—fire department T-shirts all the way to dressy button-downs. I push them aside. "What if he didn't keep the letter?"

"Don't be such a gloomy guppy!" Cricket's voice comes from the center of the dresser. "Sheesh, your mom's got a lot of underwear."

"Get out of there!" I whisper-shout.

The dresser and the wardrobe are a total bust. Not a single sign of a letter. And the longer we're in their room, the more anxious I am my parents will find us. I work quickly, but the faster I move, the more noise I make. I take on the closet next (where they usually hide Christmas and birthday presents, which they think I don't know, ha), and Cricket fishes around under the bed.

The closet is full of clothes and photo albums, ones from when Mom and Dad were kids. I'm flipping through them, hoping Dad slipped the letter from Grandpa between the pages, when Cricket calls my name. I put everything back the way I found it and rush to Dad's side of the bed. Cricket's head pokes out from under the frame. "There's a box," he says. "I think it's the one."

My heart races. "If this is it, I will love you forever."

"You don't already?"

I lie on my stomach and follow his glowing body. "Of course I do." I grab the dust-covered shoebox Cricket's hovering in front of and pull it to me. It slides across the carpet.

There's some weight to it. I wrap my fingers around the lid. "Here we go."

"Fins crossed," Cricket says.

I lift the lid. My jaw drops. "No way."

There's not a single letter inside. There's a whole *stack* of them, all addressed to Dad in the same black ink and flowy handwriting. My heart swells. All the envelopes have the same return address with the name L. Lorenzini. "This is it!" I squeak.

Grandpa didn't just write to Dad once—he's been writing to him for *years*. I pull out a handful of envelopes, shuffling through them. They're all opened. Every single one. Dad's been reading them. Why hasn't he written back? Or has he? Why hasn't he said anything? Does Mom know?

"I can't believe it," I say. "We actually found them."

"Don't just stare at them," Cricket says. "We've been in here too long for my nerves to handle. Grab one and let's get out of here."

I flip through the envelopes, find the most recent one— from about five years ago—and stuff it in my pocket. Then I shove the box back under the bed, and we scurry back to my room.

Slowly, quietly, I close my door. My hands are shaking I'm so excited. I pull the envelope from my pocket. My fingers graze the opening where the edge of the letter pokes through. "Should we read it?"

Cricket's tail flutters. "Would you want someone reading a letter *you'd* sent to someone else?"

"No," I say. "But how else are we going to figure out what's going on? The tree sent you to help me find this. We have to read it."

Cricket dips closer, poking the top corner of the envelope with his nose. "Maybe all you really need to know is how to get in touch with him. You've got that already."

"Maybe you're right." I run my thumb over the return address. "But I've got to know."

"Matteo," Cricket warns, but I'm already pulling the letter loose. I hold it to the window light. Everything around me becomes a dull hum as I read.

Dear Vinny,

I don't know what number letter this is, but I do know it'll be my last. Not because I don't want to keep writing, but because I'm afraid I've said all I can. My door is open—I will always invite you to walk through.

The most important thing is that you know how much I love you. I think about you every minute of every day. What happened between me and your mom, may she rest in peace—that was between us. Our marriage ending had nothing to do with you, but I'm afraid you felt the full brunt of my failure as a father and husband. My fear and shame led me to make many mistakes. I've gone on before about me figuring myself out, so I won't belabor it today. I just hope someday you can forgive me for not being honest sooner.

The last thing I'll say is don't forget to care for the tree in Creekside Park the way I taught you, the same way my mother and nonna taught me. That oak watches over Creekside, but our family especially. My nonna always said trees see truth because they are not bound by time as we are. They stand, unsleeping, watching everything and everyone. And they listen. They take what we breathe out and cleanse it of impurities. Trees, she said, they keep us honest. I'm afraid it didn't work on me.

My nonna also said an honest family is the strongest family. A community bound by the truest love. I failed my nonna, and I failed you. I pray that my honesty has not come too late.

All my love,

Papa

I reread the letter a dozen times more. Grandpa Ludo's words swirl in my mind. As many answers as I find in this letter, I have a hundred new questions. I am so close to finding Grandpa and figuring out why the tree is making me grow. Why it's forcing me to be so honest about everything. I can feel it.

I stash the letter under my pillow, then hunt for a piece of paper and start writing.

CREEKSIDE DOCUMENTARY TRANSCRIPT #29

SUBJECT: SERGIO GONZALEZ

. . . .

SERGIO GONZALEZ

Your mom and I, we loved taking you to the park on Sunday mornings when you were a baby. I'd pack us some scones and jelly. We'd lay out a blanket, and you'd roll around like a puppy.

AZURA GONZALEZ

What kind of scones did Mom like?

SERGIO GONZALEZ

Orange and cranberry were her favorite. Just like you.

AZURA GONZALEZ

Maybe we can take Ms. Geraldo to the park on Sunday.

SERGIO GONZALEZ

Ya know? I'd like that.

THIRTY

The rest of Tuesday passes slowly but not uneventfully. Officer James, it turns out, was only the first of many visitors to our house. Some people, like Azura and Omar, come to ask if I'm okay. Others, like Coach Mathis and the reporter from the *Creekside Herald*, come with questions, some so personal that Mom and Dad slam the door right in their faces. The worst, though, are the neighbors and other Creeksiders who show up with accusations.

"Forget the bicentennial celebration. That tree's got to come down like yesterday. I bet it's poisoning our water supply and *that*'s why your son's all messed up."

"It's his fault our tax dollars have to pay for a new library!"

"What am I supposed to do without my broom?"

With each new and more absurd claim, I realize that maybe Mom and Dad are right. At least, a little bit. I can't believe how angry people are. How afraid. How quickly they're turning on me. One man even accused my parents, saying, "The apple doesn't fall far from the tree. Your bad parenting—that's why he's messed up." Then he spat on our stoop and stomped away.

All day, I mull over what I should do. Now more than ever, it feels like it's on my shoulders to make this better. While I eat the pasta and meatballs in red sauce my parents brought up to my room for dinner, I plan with Cricket.

"I can't help anyone if I'm stuck in here," I say, chewing a mouthful of noodles.

"Now you know what it's like to live in a fishbowl," he mutters. "But where would you even go? What would you do?"

"I could find Azura. Or Omar. They usually have good ideas." I chew some more. "But I also don't want to get them in trouble. If my parents are getting this much hate from the whole town, I'm sure it won't be any better for my friends."

"What about that librarian?" Cricket asks.

I fork another noodle. "He's already been so hurt by Grandpa, and I just about killed him in the library. I don't want to drag him into this anymore."

"So that's it? You're just going to avoid people altogether?" Cricket says.

I chew. *Avoid people.* An idea forms. "Yeah, I think I am. I don't need a *person.* I need the tree. Now that we found Grandpa's letter, I bet it'll show us what to do next." What

Grandpa wrote about the oak and our family plays back in my mind. "Us Lorenzinis are tied to that tree. Grandpa's letter says so. Him leaving Creekside and me showing up— it's all connected." A zing of adrenaline makes me shiver. "I think that's why *I'm* in the middle of this whole tree-growing, lies-and-truth mess. The tree chose me to stop the lies and find the truth."

Well past midnight, after Mom and Dad are asleep, I creep downstairs. The floors wheeze underfoot, even though I pad lightly. Cricket floats just ahead of me, lighting the way. At the bottom of the stairs, I slowly turn the knob on the front door, letting in a chill draft.

"You sure about this?" Cricket whispers.

"No," I say, "but what other choice do I have?"

It's eerily quiet as we walk down the street. There are no birds or cars. Even the wind has died down. I wonder if this is what outer space is like: complete silence.

"What's it like to have feet?" Cricket asks.

Well, almost silent. "It's like having hands on your legs but less grabby."

"Hmm. I see." Cricket swishes back around. "What's it like to have hands?"

There's no one on the street, but I still look right, left, and right again before crossing to the park entrance. I'm also keeping an eye out for the police. I'll be in major trouble if

Officer James brings me home, or worse, down to the police station and my parents have to come get me!

"Can we not do twenty questions right now?" I say.

"If there's one thing I learned in my seven months, four days, six hours, and thirty-five minutes of life," says Cricket, "it's that you need to do what you want when you want. That includes asking questions. Now tell me about those hands!"

"I don't know," I say as we pass under the Creekside Park archway. "They're like power tools made of skin. Hands let you do or make pretty much anything. Hands are great."

Cricket leans in. "So you'd say they come in *handy*."

"That's literally the worst pun I've ever heard."

"*Fin*give me, but I'm just getting started."

Cue eye roll. "Come on."

When we reach the tree, I'm hit with an overwhelming rush of emotion. Guilt and relief, worry and frustration, sadness and hope. I've never felt like this before. This place, this tree—it feels different tonight. *I* feel different. The branches are thick with leaves now, dark jade in the starlit night. I place my hand on the rough bark.

I whisper, "Grandpa's letter says we're supposed to take care of you, and we didn't. But I can fix this. Show me how." A cloud passes over the moon. Everything darkens. My voice grows quieter. "I can make you better. I *can* fix this. Show me what I'm supposed to do. If you don't, they're going to cut you down after the bicentennial celebration, and that's only a couple weeks away. Everyone's so freaked out." *Me included.* I sigh. "Please. Help me."

The leaves rustle, but if they're saying something, I can't make any sense of it.

"Maybe you're not asking the right question," says Cricket.

I gaze up at the tree. "What *is* the right question?"

"That's for you to figure out." Cricket sails up into the higher branches.

"Where are you going?" I call after him. "Come back!"

But he doesn't. The park feels colder and bigger and lonelier without him at my side. So I reach for the lowest limb and climb after him. My right foot slips into an elbow of branch, and I pull myself up higher. Above me, there's a halo of light. "Cricket, wait," I call, but the light doesn't slow. It rises farther into the boughs. I grasp another limb, swatting leaves from my face.

Soon I'm so high up that I can't see the ground. But I find Cricket staring up at the moon, which almost seems within reach. I perch where three branches diverge, making a sort-of seat. Among the leaves, surrounded by boughs, it doesn't feel so chilly.

"It's beautiful," Cricket whispers, pointing to the stars with his fin. "Isn't it?"

I nod. "I don't look at the stars as much as I should."

"It's easy to forget," says Cricket, "when your whole world is a fishbowl."

I laugh. "Then what's my excuse?"

But Cricket doesn't laugh. "It's hard to look up when you're always looking in. Makes you feel small and then it's just easier to look down, isn't it?"

Wind tickles the back of my neck. "Sometimes you say big things for such a little guy."

"I do, don't I?" He sighs. "I think that's part of what makes me me. Big ideas in small packaging."

Another stretched-cotton-ball cloud passes over the moon. "What makes you you," I think aloud. My eyes fall to my hands. "I don't even know who I am. Not really."

"You're Matteo Lorenzini!" Cricket says. "Of course you know who you are."

"But where I came from, like before that night Dad found me." I pause. "My biological family hasn't mattered much to me because I've always felt like a Lorenzini. But . . . what if there's more to me? What if—what if that matters?"

"Does it *really* though?"

But now I'm spiraling down this path. I barely hear Cricket ask his question. "Maybe that *is* my problem. Maybe this isn't about me fixing the tree or Creekside or anyone. I keep trying to make my parents happy. I want to impress Omar and for Azura to always be my friend. I want the kids at school to like me. Even Tyler, if I'm being really honest."

I hug the nearest limb, resting my cheek on the gray brown bark. "But maybe it's not about what I'm supposed to do for anyone. What if . . . what if this *is* about me? What if this is all about who I am? What makes me . . . *me?*"

The wood suddenly warms under my skin. My jaw drops as the heat spills through my veins like ink in water, seeping into my every muscle and fiber. It radiates from the center of the tree—and I'm connected to all of it.

Delicate spindles of twig and leaf sprout from my arms and legs and chest. They crown my forehead and fill my hands, and every single part of me pulses with the same warmth as the tree.

"Matteo, are you okay?" Cricket asks.

But his voice is distant and muffled. Time slows, and I can't bring my lips to move or my mouth to speak. I'm becoming more tree than boy. It's taking me over—its stillness, its quiet. Its power and strength. I rest in the soft hum of its ever-expanding rings, soaking it all in. This feels familiar, like Dorothy's spoon and the family bat and even Azura's rolling pin. It feels right.

It feels like *me.*

"Cricket, I think I understand."

The fish swims closer. "What? What do you understand?"

"What's been going on with me," I say, smiling. "I know why I'm different. I thought maybe the tree was making me sick or that it made me special, but that's not it. I never was a boy to begin with." My fingers, nearly all bark now, grip the branch beneath me tighter. I laugh. "I *am* the tree."

As soon as I say the words, a gale-force wind of memory seizes me. I remember tender hands planting me two hundred years ago. A little Italian woman with bony fingers and olive skin packs earth around me. Her name comes to me: Isabetta Lorenzini. She is a strega—a witch from a land beyond the sea. She whispers something into my leaves. A prayer? A spell? No—a promise. That we shall watch over this town together. That in Creekside there will be no lies, only truth—a foundation of trust for our budding community.

I grow tall and strong for her as the years pass. Gentle rains and morning sun help me grow. Robins nest in my boughs, and squirrels tuck away their winter stores beneath my roots. I remember the seasons, the cold and the heat, how relaxing it was when I shed my leaves in autumn and the thrill of buds appearing in spring. And every year, Isabetta Lorenzini returns, until she does not, and then it's her daughters and sons, and then theirs.

Years and years pass. There are flashes of other people, their words, their hopes, their loves, their dreams. They carve their initials into my trunk; each and every letter, I wear with pride. Their cats get stuck in my branches alongside their kites and plastic bags. I relive memories of families picnicking beneath my branches and young lovers sharing a first kiss. They whisper their wants and needs, and all these years I've listened and I've watched. I've kept their truths. I've given them space beneath my branches to be themselves.

And I gave. From my very limbs, I provided for Creekside because that is what a tree does. I took the soil and rain and sunlight, and I grew and shared and loved without asking for anything in return. Yet they gave me this park to call home—they *loved* me. More memories unfurl, and my breath catches when I see a young Mr. Kowalski and another young man with olive skin—Ludo Lorenzini, my grandfather. They are both handsome. They sit close together and laugh, and my heart breaks. I see their truth, but I feel their need to lie, and it hurts me. I don't know how to help them.

Then I see my parents, each one alone, but asking for the same thing.

A child.

A child, a child, a child.

After I failed to help Ludo see his truth, I had to do whatever I could for his son and daughter-in-law. It all makes so much sense now. I was willing to do anything to make it right. That's why the last gift I ever gave as a tree was the gift of myself, my very heart and soul.

The only thing, I realize now, is that it wasn't just a gift for Mom and Dad. It was for me too. For so long I watched

Creekside flourish. I'd held Creeksiders' lives in my leaves, and now I wanted a chance to live a human life. To play and laugh and walk among them. To share *my* truth. To make friends. To love as people do. That was my honest wish. So on a bright, starlit night, I poured out every bit of magic the strega poured into me and became a tree *and* a baby, nestled in a wooden basket on the front steps of the Creekside Fire Department.

As quickly as it began, the flood of memory fades to a trickle. I breathe deeply and open my eyes. The sky is pink with dawn. A robin chirps below me. The heat from the tree diminishes, retreating until the faintest warmth dances below my fingertips, where my skin meets the soft bark.

My eyes narrow. Something's wrong. The oak's bark— *my* bark—has turned white as paper, and the branches are bare. All the newly grown leaves are gone.

Then I notice the sound. A siren like a fire engine. "Cricket, what is that?"

He hovers nearby, fins wringing together nervously. "I really hope you got the answers you need because we've got company, and they do *not* look happy."

CREEKSIDE DOCUMENTARY TRANSCRIPT #30

SUBJECT: JENNIFER JONES

. . . .

JENNIFER JONES

Omar talks about you all the time. He just adores you and Matteo. Anyhoo, what can I help you with, sweetheart?

AZURA GONZALEZ

I just want to know what you think about this whole tree situation.

JENNIFER JONES

The one in the park? Oh, I'm glad they're cutting it down after the big celebration. Thing's an eyesore. I just hope they replace it with something special. I love running in the park. Wouldn't mind a fountain or something.

AZURA GONZALEZ

You won't miss the tree at all?

JENNIFER JONES

A little, I suppose, but we put too much emphasis on tradition in this town. This town could use some rejuvenating.

THIRTY-ONE

Peering down between the thick branches, I see the shapes of people moving around. Engines whine in the air. *Weee-ooo, weee-ooo, weee-ooo.* "My parents must have found out I was missing," I say, stretching my sore muscles. "I didn't think I'd be gone this long."

I scurry down faster than I climbed up. I wonder if getting around a tree is easier now because I know what I really am. It's weird to think I'm climbing myself. I guess it could also be the daylight speeding up my descent . . . Whatever the case, I leap from the last bough to the dewy grass, and I'm immediately tackled by Mom's suffocating embrace. "Matteo! We were so worried."

Dad is there too, in his firehouse T-shirt and jeans, looking very concerned.

"Mm fime," I mumble, smothered by Mom's chest. She finally lets up. I gulp in air, but my pulse quickens when I see what's happening.

The oak tree is surrounded by Creeksiders. Some, like Mrs. Mandrake and Ms. Grainger, are still in their pajamas and robes. Officer James is furiously pacing, telling folks to back up, including Azura and Omar, who are trying to push past a barricade of yellow caution tape that now rings the tree. The most alarming are the men and women in hard hats holding chainsaws. I recognize a couple of them from the fire department.

"What are they doing?" I ask.

"Oh, honey," Mom says. "There is something horribly wrong with the tree. The bark's gone white and it's ooz-ing black sap." She points at the dark, gaping wound along the trunk. It's even uglier now that the bark's lost its hue. But now I know why the tree's dying. I spent too much of myself—as a tree and a boy—trying to fix everything. I'm not sick. I'm worn out, and I've been trying to do everything on my own. But my brain can't put my thoughts into words fast enough. Mom goes on, "And the town is going wild. More wooden objects are coming alive all over the place, and people are in a frenzy!" She smooths my hair. "When we didn't find you in your bed, we knew you must have come here."

Dad leans down. He holds me firmly by the shoulders. "That tree is dangerous, Matteo. I get it now. All our prob-lems, everything that's gone wrong—it all comes back to this tree. I called the mayor's office this morning. They agreed that we don't need to wait until after the bicentennial celebration. It's got to come down. Now."

My heart nearly stops. "No! You can't. You don't understand!"

"It's been decided," he says, walking away from me.

He nods at one of the women in a hard hat. She yanks the pull cord on her chainsaw. It rumbles to life, the blades whirring along the metal oval.

"You can't do this!" I scream. I'm so close to fixing everything.

Another chainsaw revs. Fear crawls across my skin. I try to break free from Mom's grip, but she holds tighter. "Let me go!" Officer James forces the Creeksiders farther back. Now, accompanied by the sound of blades, the people gathered around listen. Even Azura and Omar shuffle down the hill.

"Matteo, stop," Mom says. "This is for the best."

"You don't know what's for the best. They can't do this!" I don't want to know what will happen to me if they chop down *my* tree. But there's no time to explain. "You're making a huge mistake. Please, listen to me!"

Dad looks me in the eye. "You need to listen to me. I know this tree is special to you, but I can't take another day of watching you suffer. This is how it's gotta be." His voice softens. "Matteo, we're doing this for you."

Mom leans in. "You're our world. We love you so, *so* much. We just want you safe."

Words stick in my throat. They say they love me, but they have no idea that they're loving me the wrong way. This will destroy me.

Before I can respond, the first chainsaw rips into the oak. Pain like heartache seizes in my chest. I crumple forward. My parents catch me as I fall, but they don't understand. I gasp for air. *Please, someone, stop the saws!* I'm shouting but the words don't come out. Anguish cleaves my heart in two as the blades go deeper.

"It's okay," Mom whispers. "Everything will be okay."

I cry into her arms. Everything hurts, from my toenails to the tips of my hair. I can't catch my breath. Dad's hand rests on my head like a helmet, but it feels more like it's crushing my skull.

It's over in a matter of minutes, but every second is excruciating. The oak groans, an aching, soul-suffering moan. I moan with it. Then the tree tilts backward. Birds flee from the upper branches. Squirrels scurry down the trunk, leaping for the ground. And like a slain giant, it thunders to the earth.

I shudder. The saws go silent.

And then the crowd does too. Slowly, Creeksiders disappear, back to homes and shops, back to school and work, back to gardens and front porches.

I am a heap on the ground between Mom and Dad. They whisper in my ear. They tell me everything will be all right, but even with them beside me, I have never felt so alone. When I finally stop crying, they help me up and take me away under an overcast sky just as the first trickles of rain fall on our heads.

CREEKSIDE DOCUMENTARY TRANSCRIPT #31

SUBJECT: MILES SUDBURY

· ·

MILES SUDBURY

I don't believe in magic. Those stories going around town, about that tree? It's all hokey.

AZURA GONZALEZ

Why don't you think magic exists?

MILES SUDBURY

Magic is an excuse, an easy way out. I love my Creekside, but too many people around here get distracted by fairy tales. The truth is life is full of joy and heartache. And in the middle there's a lot of hard work. Not magic. Just grit.

THIRTY-TWO

For two whole days, I refuse to get out of bed. With the tree gone, I'm terrified about what will happen to me. I feel hollow—like I'm only half of myself. I'm so weak. I worry my legs will give out if I try to stand.

Maybe *refuse* is the wrong word then. I'm *incapable* of moving. My limbs are lead. My brain is mush. A cloudy haze fuzzes over my vision. Even Cricket, who's thankfully still around despite the tree getting cut down, can't seem to motivate me. On the third day, though, I muster my courage and drag myself downstairs. A dull headache pings behind my eyes.

"Hey, bud," Dad says, sipping a cup of coffee. "How're you feeling?"

"Like there's a chainsaw in my brain."

He doesn't ask me anything for a while after that. Both my parents pick up that I'm not in the mood for questions.

The furious grief and pain I felt when they chopped down my tree has simmered into concentrated anger and nausea. All I can think about is how Mom and Dad, the people who say they love me most, didn't listen. How they chose to believe fear and other people over me.

Later that afternoon, Azura and Omar stop by. I bring them up to my room, and this time I make a point to close the door. I don't care what the rules are. This is the first time I've seen anyone other than Mom, Dad, or Cricket in days. Right now, I need my friends more than anything. They're the only people who really get me.

"We've been so worried," Azura says. "What they did to the tree . . . it was awful. I'm so sorry."

"Yeah," Omar agrees. "I was worried we'd never see you again. School's not the same without you. Are you ever coming back?"

"Next week, maybe," I say. "I miss you guys, but I'm a mess. Not 'sick' though. My blood tests came back totally normal. Dr. Wilson says I don't need to quarantine. Of course, Mom and Dad are convinced cutting down the tree is what helped, but that's not it. I've always been fine." I pause, looking at my bed. "There is something I need to tell you though. Cricket, you wanna help?"

He emerges from under the bed. "Greetings, Matteo's friends!"

Azura yelps. Omar squeaks, "What is that?"

"I think you mean 'who'?" Cricket corrects. "I'm Cricket, the friendly ghostfish, formerly a goldfish."

Omar rubs his eyes. "How is the ghost of your goldfish in your room? I thought all the weird things stopped when they cut down the tree."

"They did," Azura says. "All over town, things have gone back to the way they were. No more runaway ladders or root-tentacled rolling pins. I don't understand."

Omar brightens. "Does that mean you still have your tree superpowers?"

Cricket and I share a look. "There's something we need to tell you. Something *big*," I say. "Other than Cricket, you are the only people alive—"

Cricket coughs into his fin. "Not alive. Or a 'people.'"

"Fine. The only *two living people* who will know the truth about me."

My friends lean in closer.

"When I climbed the oak the other night, I—" I pause. What if *being* a tree isn't as cool as having tree *powers?*

"What?" Omar says.

Azura adds, "You can tell us."

I relax a little. They've been with me this far. What's one more weirdness? So I say, "I saw things. Memories. Things about who I am. Who I *really* am. I thought I was connected to the tree, but the truth is, I *am* the tree."

Their jaws drop. Then Azura's and Omar's lips twist,

like they're trying to form words, but they don't say any-thing. I squirm. This isn't the "oh you're a magic superhero" reaction I was hoping for. I fight the urge to run away. Maybe I shouldn't have told them.

"Can you believe it?" Cricket says, cutting the tension. "Almost as shocking as me!"

"But . . . *how?*" Azura finally says.

Taking a deep breath to calm my nerves, I do my best to explain what I saw in the tree. About the strega and the promise she and I made to each other. How I watched over Creekside for almost two hundred years. How I wished to be human and that's how I became a boy.

When I finish, Omar smirks. "Sooo . . . you're kind of like the Little Mermaid?"

I scratch the back of my neck, laughing. "Yeah, I guess, just not as pretty."

"You're not *not* pre—" He stops abruptly. "I mean, you look—"

My skin tingles. Was Omar about to say what I think he's saying? Ohmygod. But Azura butts in, tucking a strand of hair behind her ear. "Okay, so, if they cut the tree down, what does that mean for you? Like . . ."

Dark realization squishes Omar's face. "Are you going to die?"

I hug my knees to my chest. "Maybe? I don't know. I don't think so. But I haven't felt like myself since. It's like

I'm empty on the inside. Only half of who I used to be."

"That sucks," says Omar. "But I'm glad you're still here."

Azura props herself up on her knees. "How can we help? There's got to be a way to make you whole again."

"Well, I *had* a plan to save the tree." I tell them about finding Grandpa Ludo's letters and writing to him. How I hoped he would come back and tell me how to heal the oak. "But what good is any of that if all we've got is a stump? It's not like we can bring a tree back to life."

"But *you're* alive," says Omar. "If *you're* the tree, doesn't that mean it's still alive?"

The first spark of hope I've felt in days lights in my chest. "I didn't think about that."

"As a ghost," Cricket says, "I can vouch for the existence of half-living things."

"But even if the tree is still alive," Azura says, "how do you regrow a tree from a stump? Is that even possible?"

Omar twists one of his hair curls. "Azura, we're talking to a tree boy and a ghost goldfish. I'm pretty sure anything is possible."

"I prefer *ghostfish*, actually," Cricket says.

"Maybe you're right." I smile. "Maybe anything is possible."

· ·

CHELSEA GERALDO

Out with the old, in with the new. Now that we're coming up on the bicentennial celebration, I think it's about time!

AZURA GONZALEZ

Why do you say that?

CHELSEA GERALDO

It's always the same thing in Creekside! We need new. We need fresh.

AZURA GONZALEZ

Like new boyfriends?

CHELSEA GERALDO

What? No! I'm not letting your dad get away from me.

AZURA GONZALEZ

Oh good. This would be a terrible way for him to find out you're breaking up.

CHELSEA GERALDO

We're not breaking up!

THIRTY-THREE

Mom's all sunshine and butterflies on Saturday morning. "Dr. Wilson says you're able to play again, so let's get you back out there and make the best of things!"

"Just think about how great you played last game." Dad frowns. "Well, aside from the whole bat thing."

"Trust us," Mom says cheerily. "This'll get you out of your slump."

We're sitting around the kitchen table. I'm (reluctantly) dressed in my Blue Whales jersey and baseball pants, freshly bleached white. Aside from the fact that I still feel like crap, I know the whole town has been talking about me. How Mom and Dad expect me to show my face in public, let alone play a game, is beyond me. They're acting like everything is normal again, but they're kidding themselves.

"It'll be good for you to get out and stretch," Mom says. She sets a plate of buttered toast in front of me. "Move the muscles. That's what my mother always told me to do when I was feeling low."

I wave my arms over my head. "I'm moving them."

She purses her lips. "Very funny."

"What if I don't go?" I chomp into a piece of toast, watching their faces for a reaction.

"Then I don't see how you can go to school on Monday," Dad says. "You're playing today and getting back into the swing of things. No buts."

"That's not fair," I say. "Baseball and school aren't the same thing."

Mom takes my hand in hers. "We're just trying to help you. Now that you're not . . . changing anymore, you need to start living again."

I pull my hand back. "I *am* living. I was before too."

Dad swirls his coffee. Steam spirals upward. "We're not arguing about this. You're going." Then he gets up, dumps the rest of his coffee into the sink, and heads out the door.

I plead with Mom. "Please don't make me go."

"Sometimes we have to do things we don't want to do." She pinches my cheek. "It'll be good for you." She grabs her purse from the counter. "Bring that last piece of toast with you."

I begrudgingly stuff the crust between my teeth, grab my gear, and follow her out the door. I wonder how much longer I'm supposed to trust them before they trust me.

* * *

The field is damp. Grass squishes under my shoes. Today we're up against the Amber Owls, a wily bunch of kids from a town over who seem to think everything is a joke. Even their own coach, a tall white woman with chestnut hair pulled into a ponytail, seems to be annoyed with them. I'm already anxious, but when one of their players asks me if I'm "that bark boy" he heard about, I start to shake. I retreat to the bench, pretending I didn't hear him. *Everyone* knows about me, even people outside of Creekside. They all think I'm a freak.

Mom and Dad were so wrong. I never should have come today.

And things only get worse. Aside from Omar, the Blue Whales act so distant around me, I might as well be on another planet. "Don't let Tyler and the other guys get to you," Omar whispers in my ear at the top of the third inning. "They're more intimidated by you than anything."

That surprises me. "Pretty sure you've got that wrong."

"No, for real," he says. "Everyone knows you're special. That makes you better than them, and that freaks them out."

"You're saying they're jealous?" I laugh. "No way. I'm not better than anybody."

Omar winks. "I call it like I see it."

He can't be right. Omar's just trying to cheer me up. But the idea that people might not think I'm a total mutant weirdo does make me feel a little better. Especially coming from him.

The Blue Whales get their third out before I have to bat, which is a relief, and I run to left field slightly more encouraged than before. Maybe there is something to what Mom said. About moving the muscles. Or maybe it's being around Omar, who actually gets me.

Still, as I stand in the misting rain, I feel like I'm only half there. Part of my mind is with the stump in Creekside Park. I wonder if I'll ever really, truly feel whole again.

It's only a matter of minutes before the bases are loaded with Amber Owls. Tyler's been pitching, but he's off his game. And he's hocking loogies more than usual. He's definitely frustrated.

I squeeze my fingers in my glove, punching the center of the mitt. I tug my cap tight around my head. As terrible as I feel, maybe I can be the one to turn this game around.

That's it. If that ball comes anywhere near me, I'm going to catch it.

Mom gives me a thumbs-up from the stands, her poncho slick with water. Dad's on his feet next to her, hands in his pockets, shouting, "You got this, Matteo! Get that mitt ready!"

Tyler goes into his windup, then spins forward and a white lightning blur races toward the Amber Owl at home plate. I hold my breath.

Smack!

The Amber Owl bolts as the ball soars into the air. My knees bend. It's coming straight for me.

"Mitt up, Matteo!" Coach Mathis shouts. "Hustle after it!"

My legs pump beneath me, my heart jackhammering in my ears. My head turns to the gray sky. There it is, almost directly above me: a white fleck, a freckle, a pinprick. *I can do this. I can do this.* Then it's sinking, plummeting—

"Run, Matteo, RUN!"

I lunge, my body launching over the ground, suspended in time, left arm reaching, reaching, reaching. In the instant before my body hits the ground, I feel the satisfying punch of the baseball falling into—

Snnnick!

I land hard on the ground. My teeth grind together. My head lolls. Something's wrong. I expect a rush of pain, the blistering fire of broken bones, but I feel . . . nothing.

I sit up. My left shoulder feels strange. Lighter.

The crowd shouts, "Throw in the ball!"

I shake the daze from my head. *I caught it, didn't I?*

The crowd hollers louder for me to move. The Amber Owl who'd been on third is halfway home. I've got to hurry. *The ball, the ball, the—*

My eyes widen. My stomach flops. Lying in the grass, completely severed from the rest of me, is my left arm, the baseball planted in the glove.

My arm broke off.

My arm *broke off.*

There's a tidal wave in my stomach. The fingers on my right hand travel along the empty space where my left arm had been. I'm going to be sick. *That* was the sound. My arm snapping from the rest of me like a carrot cracking in two, which isn't possible—*shouldn't* be possible.

Coach Mathis's voice slices through my thoughts. "The ball, Matteo! The ball!"

I caught the ball. Not in a hand still attached to the rest of me, but I caught it.

I push myself to standing, praying I don't hurl. Then I bend low and scoop up my broken arm, my mitt, and the ball. Embarrassment and shock burn in my cheeks as I run toward the pitcher's mound.

But it's too late. The last of the three Amber Owls runs through home plate, their fans hooting in delight. I want to cry. I failed. Again. And I'm broken worse than I ever was. Even though I did exactly what my parents wanted today, it still wasn't enough. *I'm* not enough.

Now that I'm closer to the crowd, a wail silences the cheers. "His—his *arm!*" A pale woman in a ruby raincoat gasps, her finger jabbing toward me.

White-hot shivers climb over my back and shoulders as the crowd turns to look at me. My knees wobble. There's the briefest moment of shocked silence, and then everyone is shouting. Even from across the field, I feel Mom's eyes reaching for me, holding me too close. But the tightening circle of boys and coaches block my parents from view. I shrink into myself. Among the concerned and confused faces are those that seem disturbed and disgusted.

"What a freak," Tyler whispers to Miguel Ruiz. Jimmy Briar stares unblinking at the broken arm I'm holding in my other hand. Then he turns around and throws up.

Only Omar asks me if I'm all right, but he sounds afraid. I don't blame him. I'm majorly terrified. I never thought I'd break the way a tree does. But now that it's happened, it's like I should have known it could happen all along.

"Everyone, back up," Dad shouts, barreling through the circle.

Mom is right behind him. She cups my face in her hands. "What happened?"

I can't meet her eyes. "I—I don't know. It just . . . came off."

A tear balances on the edge of my eyelid, but before it falls, she thumbs it away, whispering, "You are okay. You will be okay." She wraps me in her arms, the broken limb sandwiched between us. "It's all right," she says. "It'll be all right. We'll get you to Dr. Wilson straightaway."

I want to hide in her arms forever, but when I look up, there's Tyler with his perfectly normal arms—the ones that throw and catch and swing. He's the boy my parents wish they had. Not me. He catches me staring and backs away, whispering something ugly to Miguel.

I feel hot and sick and small. This game was supposed to make me feel better, but it's made everything a million times worse. Dad is still shouting for everyone to stand back. Some of the parents pull their kids away, but more watch with horrified fascination. Dad turns fire hydrant red. "Give us some freaking space," he shouts, and finally the crowd retreats.

I clutch my broken arm to my chest. I'm so confused. There isn't any blood. No bones sticking out. No pain. Only emptiness. Hollowness. I turn the arm so I can see the spot where it snapped off. My breath becomes thick as sap in my throat. Where there should be bone and muscle, there's only sand-colored wood and brown rings within rings within rings.

Mom's hand hovers in front of her mouth. "Oh my god."

I look up at her. "Do you see me now?"

CREEKSIDE DOCUMENTARY TRANSCRIPT #33

SUBJECT: MAISY PATEL

· ·

MATTEO LORENZINI

What's your experience with the tree in Creekside Park?

MAISY PATEL

I like to climb it. Especially in the fall, when the leaves are gone and I can see for miles. There's nothing else like it.

MATTEO LORENZINI

What do you see when you're up there?

MAISY PATEL

Everything. All at once. All of Creekside. From so high up, it's so much easier to see how everything is connected.

THIRTY-FOUR

Dr. Wilson has already come and gone. She was waiting at our door when we got home from the game. She took one look at me and said, "Now this I have never seen before."

"Can you help him?" Mom asked.

"Help him?" Dr. Wilson replied. "I don't even know how to diagnose him. Whatever's happening here"—she waved her hand over my brokenness—"*this* is a biological wonder, and I work in science, not miracles." And then she left with my broken-off arm in a biohazard bag, muttering to herself.

Miracles. That word has bounced in my mind ever since. I don't feel like a miracle.

I *need* a miracle.

Around dinnertime, Mom reheats some homemade baked mostaccioli from the freezer. Usually, the smell of red sauce and ricotta puts me at ease, but I'm numb to it all. I'm not even hungry, and I haven't had a bite since this morning.

"Matteo, I—" Dad says, rubbing the stubble on his chin.

"I keep trying to make sense of it all, what's happening to you, but I just can't."

My finger traces a gouge in the table. "It's like you said. I'm unwell." I look at him. "Congratulations. Turns out you were right all along."

Mom brings the steaming pan of cheesy pasta to the table and takes a seat. "We didn't want to be right, and this isn't what we meant. Not at all." Her eyes dart to my armless shoulder. "We had no idea what was happening inside you."

I stare at my empty plate. "I tried to tell you."

"Matteo, you have to—" Dad sighs. "You're right. You did try."

"I—I didn't want to believe it could be true," Mom says sadly.

Dad clears his throat. "I was just so scared for you. I didn't understand what the tree had done. I still don't. I really, truly thought we were helping you when we cut it down, but now . . ." He reaches for my hand. "God. I'm scared I did the very thing I set out not to do. That *we've* broken you. That this *is* our fault—" He chokes on the words. "And now, I really don't know how to help you."

"Neither of us do." Mom stretches her hand across the table, caressing my cheek. "We really did try our best."

Did you though? I want to ask. But I don't have the energy to argue, so I say, "I wish—I wish I didn't have to break for you to get it."

Mom wipes away a tear. "Us too, baby. Us too."

"How can we make this right? I'll do anything," Dad says.

Mom leans on Dad's shoulder. "*We'll* do anything."

These are the words I wish they'd said days ago. I'm worried it's too late. "I don't know what to do yet," I say, "but I want to tell you the truth about me. For real. I know it's going to sound strange, but you promise to listen?"

"We promise," Mom says.

Dad nods.

"And you promise not to freak out?"

Dad laughs darkly. "Don't think you can freak me out much more than I already am, sport."

I roll my eyes. "We'll see about that." I tilt my head back and call, "Cricket!"

The little ghostfish zooms through the wall and into the kitchen. Mom and Dad recoil in their seats.

"What the—" Dad starts, then stops himself. "What's going on, Matteo?"

"I want to introduce a friend of mine," I say.

Cricket tips his head to my parents. "Pleasure to finally meet you both. I'm Cricket, Matteo's ghostfish, confidant, and the greatest being to ever exist."

"Don't push it," I mumble.

He rolls his eyes. "Fine. The greatest *ghostfish* to ever exist."

"Cricket?" Mom says, eyes turning to me. "As in your goldfish? The one that died?"

"The very same," Cricket replies.

"But how?" Dad asks.

"The oak," I say. "In Creekside Park. When I buried Cricket under the tree, it gave him a new life, sort of. The tree's been taking care of Creeksiders, watching over us and helping where it can, for as long as it's existed." Now I look directly at Dad. "Isn't that right?"

"That's what my father told me growing up." His forehead creases. "But those were just stories. I thought—"

"Not just stories, Dad." I'm not quite ready to bring up Grandpa yet. One thing at a time. "It's all true."

His eyebrows furrow. "So you're saying, that day, when your mom and I went to the tree asking for a child, it *found* you for us? It wasn't a coincidence?"

"No, it wasn't a coincidence. But the oak didn't find me." I take a deep breath. They've got to be able to hear my heart beating, it's so loud. I speak slowly. "I *am* the tree."

My parents squint, absorbing the news.

"You . . . are . . . the tree?" Mom says.

"And a boy," I add quickly.

"You're a boy *and* a tree." Dad pinches the bridge of his nose. "But . . . how? What does that even mean?"

"All my life, when I was just a tree, people came to me with wishes and dreams," I say, trying to remember what

I saw the night I climbed the oak. My tree memories are cloudy, but if I concentrate hard enough, they sharpen into focus. "I watched other people live for so long. I was so full of human hopes and wants and needs that I started to have my own. When you both came to me, it felt like an opportunity, not just to give something to you but to myself. Instead of watching, I could *do* something. So I made my wish to be human." I look at both of them. "And to be your son."

Mom wipes away another tear. "Why? Why ours?"

"You both had so much love to give." I close my eyes, recalling the memory of them. "I can still feel it. How strong it was." I open my eyes. "How strong it is."

"We do love you," Dad says. "So much."

I shift awkwardly in my chair. He's saying it, but I'm still not sure he loves *all* of me. "I know. I do too."

"Thank you for choosing us," Mom says.

"Thank you for choosing me," I say.

"I really am taking this all in," says Dad. "But what do we do now? You trusted us, and all we've done is hurt you."

"Cricket and I think there must be some magic left in the stump," I say. "But it's getting less and less. I think that's why I'm alive but my arm broke off."

Cricket flails his fins. "And I'm literally fading away. I barely have my signature glow!"

"If he disappears, I might be next." My shoulders sag. "What if I turn into a pile of mulch?"

262

"That stump's our only hope," Cricket adds. "If there's no way to save it, we're already sardines in a can. And time's not on our side."

"We can't let that happen. There must be a way," Mom says.

"We'll do whatever it takes," Dad adds.

"Thanks." I grin. I hope Dad really means it, because I've already set something in motion that he might not like. My stomach gurgles. Maybe I can save that news for tomorrow.

"Why don't we take a beat and have some dinner?" For the first time all day, Dad smiles. "It'll do us all some good."

Mom scoops a heaping mound of pasta, white mozzarella stringing from the pan, onto all our plates. "My nonna always said a little food can do wonders."

I eat a forkful. "That's just what we need."

CREEKSIDE DOCUMENTARY TRANSCRIPT #34

SUBJECT: MAYOR MEYERS

• •

MAYOR MEYERS

I do everything I can to protect this town. Whatever it takes. I trust my law enforcement to ensure that happens.

MATTEO LORENZINI

Does anything bad ever even happen in Creekside?

MAYOR MEYERS

Not under my watch.

THIRTY-FIVE

With everything being so weird, I'm craving something normal. So Monday morning, I go to school, despite Mom and Dad's hesitation.

"What about your, um, *arm*?" Mom asks. She still makes a face every time she looks at my empty shoulder. "Is it safe for you to go like that?"

"I'll be okay." Uncomfortable with her stare, I cover my shoulder with my right hand. "I've been practicing using one arm. Trust me."

Before I leave, Dad gingerly pins up the empty sleeve where my arm should be. I'm not sure if he means to or not, but he backs away quick when he's done. "We trust you, but we also know how kids can be. If you need to come home, call us. We'll pick you up."

"Thanks." They wrap their arms awkwardly around me. My own is trapped at my side.

Azura and Omar are waiting outside my door. They don't say anything as they stare at my armless shoulder.

"You can ask me about it," I say.

Omar holds his own arm like he's afraid it'll fall off too. "Does it hurt?"

"Yes and no," I say. "It's not a body pain. More like a heart pain. If that makes sense."

Azura nods. "A piece of you is missing. That's how I felt when Mom died."

"Right," I say, smiling sadly. "And I don't know how to be whole again. I was actually hoping you two could help me come up with a plan."

Omar swings his arm around my neck. He pulls me close. My chest flutters as he says, "Whatever you need, boss."

"We've got you," says Azura.

I feel a little better having my friends at my side, but when we turn the corner onto Main Street, something feels off. Downtown Creekside—Conehead's, the mayor's office, the Gonzalez's bakery—everything's the same, but the air is heavy, like the buildings are holding their breath. Other kids on their way to school don't laugh or joke as loud as they usually do. Or maybe I'm just imagining it?

But then Omar says, "It's too quiet. I don't like it."

A shiver runs down my back. "I was thinking the same thing!"

"Did we miss something?" Azura says. She waves at

Maisy and Lillian, who're walking across the street from us, but they don't wave back. In fact, they seem to intentionally *ignore* Azura. She drops her hand and says, "Okay. *Rude*. Why're they acting so weird?"

But it's obvious to me, and I'm a little surprised it isn't to her. "You're with *me*, Azura. *I'm* what's weird." I point to the space where my left arm should be.

Her face falls. "Oh." She quickly adjusts her disappointment into a frown. "Well, they're still rude!"

I look up and down the sidewalk. None of the other kids on their way to school will meet my gaze. Ugh. Maybe leaving home was a bad idea. "It feels like the whole town is against me now," I say.

As if in response, the sidewalk rumbles and a crack appears beneath our feet. A hairline gap shoots forward. A brown root pokes out. Azura, Omar, and I leap out of its way.

"Whoa," Omar shouts. "Did you just do that?"

"Wasn't me." I dance around the crack. "At least, I don't think it was." A chill wind blows by, one much too cold for it to be nearly May. My eyes linger on the root. A new idea hits me. "Me and the tree and Creekside, we're all connected, right? What if—what if they didn't just hurt *me* when they chopped down the oak? What if they hurt the whole town, and they didn't even realize they were doing it?"

Azura pales. She combs her hair behind her ears. "Let's just get to school."

Creekside Middle School is just as awkward as the rest of town. When we walk in, kids and teachers are milling around, some talking, others laughing and then stopping themselves. Some point at me. I duck behind Azura and Omar, using them as shields. I thought being here would make me feel normal, but I was *so* wrong.

Tyler passes by, and I brace for some insult, but he just looks grossed out, which almost feels worse than him calling me "Matty" or "wuss."

"I'm not complaining that he didn't make fun of me," I whisper to Azura and Omar, "but ignoring me? Is that a new low?"

"He's still being a jerk," says Azura. She looks around. "Honestly, this whole place is giving me bad vibes."

The bad vibes continue all day. I make a point to pass by the library on my way to lunch. The lights are off, and the doors are barricaded. A hastily made DO NOT ENTER sign is taped to each of the double doors. The words are double underlined in red marker. I wonder where Mr. Kowalski is. Maybe he stayed home. Without a library, what does a librarian do?

Guilt crawls under my skin. I wish I could apologize. I never meant to hurt anything or anyone, especially Mr. Kowalski. Not after how Grandpa Ludo already hurt him. There's a tug at my heart. I think again about the letter I wrote. Even though it's too late to save the tree, I wonder if Grandpa got it. Would he even bother to read it after all this time? I hope so.

I tough out the school day, but I'm drained by the time the last bell rings. It's exhausting being immersed in all this heaviness, especially when I'm already weighed down.

"You don't look so good," Azura says while we're at her locker. She shoves papers into the bottom of her bag.

"It's been a long day," I say.

She zips the lip of her bag shut. "Want to come to the bakery with me? I'm helping Dad out so he can get ready for a date with Ms. Geraldo. Treats usually make you feel better."

I appreciate her trying, but that's not what I need. "I'm just gonna go home."

"You sure?"

"I'm sure."

I walk home alone, taking a slightly different path, my thumb under the shoulder strap of my backpack. It helps keep it in place with my one arm gone.

My feet walk as if they have a mind of their own. It isn't long before I'm standing at the entrance to Creekside Park. So many emotions stir inside me but mostly grief. If only I could go back in time, when my tree still watched over everything.

I've almost convinced myself to keep walking home when there's a tug at my feet. An inexplicable urge to go into the park. *No*, I tell myself. *It'll only hurt you to see what's left*. But there's another feeling pushing back against my sadness. It's hard to name it at first, but then I realize what's driving me to the remains of the old oak.

It's hope.

CREEKSIDE DOCUMENTARY TRANSCRIPT #35

SUBJECT: JENNIE O'CONNOR

· ·

JENNIE O'CONNOR

I've never told anyone this, but sometimes I have dreams about the tree. But it's only after I've had a nightmare. It's like the oak chases away the bad thoughts. Is that strange?

AZURA GONZALEZ

Nothing's strange at this point. How long has that been going on?

JENNIE O'CONNOR

Oh, gosh. All my life? I guess it won't happen anymore, will it?

THIRTY-SIX

I'm not prepared to see someone else standing next to the stump. I hang back, scrutinizing him. He's tall, wearing a tan windbreaker and khaki pants. The stranger hunches slightly, starting at his shoulders. His neck cranes over what's left of my tree.

I'd been feeling hopeful, but my nerves ramp up again seeing this person here. What if I was wrong? What if something even worse is about to happen? But I can't ignore the itch in my feet, this magnetism drawing me back.

I inch closer, one timid step at a time. The nearer I get, the more I can make out of him. He is an older white man with olive skin. His cheeks are dotted with well-tended gray stubble. Deep lines grace the corners of his eyes, but his lips are firmly set. When I get to the opposite side of the stump, he looks up, surprised. "Hello," he says.

"Hello."

His eyes linger where my left arm should be, then they

272

dart to my face. He points a craggy finger. "Do you know what happened to this tree?"

"They cut it down last week." My voice catches in my throat. "It was dying. Weird things were happening around town. They thought getting rid of it would help."

He sighs heavily. "I wish they hadn't. I wish—I should have been here."

He is so familiar, but I can't place where I've seen him. "Are you from Creekside?"

"I was," he says. "A long, long time ago." His gaze wanders up, into the empty space where the oak's trunk should be. "This tree was always one of my happiest places."

My head suddenly aches. The sound of his voice . . . I *know* it. I rub the back of my skull, soothing the pain. "What did you say your name was?"

"I didn't," he chuckles softly. "You can call me—"

"Ludo?"

I freeze, finally putting it all together. *Ludo. Ohmygosh, ohmygosh, ohmygosh!* That's why he's so familiar; he's my grandpa! He must have gotten my letter!

We both turn at the sound of his name. Slightly downhill stands Mr. Kowalski. He is wax white. The hand on his cane shakes.

"Kaz." Grandpa Ludo says Mr. Kowalski's nickname like it's a delicate flower.

I can't believe what I'm seeing. It seems they can't either.

273

They're still as statues, staring at each other for an eternity.

And then they are running to each other. I've never seen old people full-out run, but Mr. Kowalski and Grandpa Ludo sprint into each other's arms. Their heads tuck into the other's shoulder, and they shake. They hold each other. Something between laughter and sobs comes out of both of them. They pull back, gaze into the other's face, and embrace again.

"What are you doing here?" Mr. Kowalski finally asks. "*How* are you here?"

Grandpa Ludo wipes the other man's face with a handkerchief. "I got a letter from a grandson I've never met. His name's—"

"Matteo," I say, finding my voice. On wobbly legs, I step closer. "That's me."

Grandpa Ludo collapses to his knees, all smiles. He grabs me by the shoulders, and I teeter, off-balance in his grip. "Oh, Matteo. Look at you!" He cups my cheek in his dry palm. "Thank you for writing to me."

Mr. Kowalski clears his throat. "I thought I'd never see you again. How did he find you?"

"My son apparently kept my letters," Grandpa Ludo says, standing. "Matteo found them. He wrote to me and explained everything that's been going on, though it seems the situation has gotten far worse since you wrote."

"Much, much worse," I say. "I'm so glad you're here."

Grandpa Ludo tilts his head to Mr. Kowalski and says, "You know, my son's not the only person in Creekside I tried writing to."

Mr. Kowalski pales and quickly takes Grandpa Ludo's hand. "I'm sorry I never wrote you back, Ludo. I was so angry and hurt and confused. When I finally made peace with it all, I felt like I was too late."

"Oh, Kaz. I'm sorry too." He places his other hand on top of Mr. Kowalski's. My heart hurts watching them. They waited *so* long to find each other again, to be honest with each other. I know we're just kids, but I don't want that to happen with me and Omar. If I never say how I really feel, will I end up saying something too late? Will I regret not being honest sooner? My toes curl in my shoes at the thought.

Then Grandpa looks back and forth between me and the librarian. "How did you two know I'd be here?"

I bite my lip, not quite sure how to answer, but Mr. Kowalski's gaze falls to the stump. He says, "I didn't. I've been coming here every day since they cut the oak down. The tree was dying, and Creekside was out of sorts, but that doesn't change what that tree meant to me. What it meant to us."

Explaining why *I'm* here is too much to get into right now, but I say, "Grandpa, there's got to be a way to save the oak. I know about the strega planting the tree and how we were supposed to take care of it, but then we didn't, and I tried to fix everything myself, and—"

"Matteo's had a rough few weeks," Mr. Kowalski interjects. He shuffles toward me. "You and this tree, you've got a special connection to it, like us. Don't you?"

I nod, unsure how much I should say in front of Mr. Kowalski.

"Must have hurt you to see it come down," Grandpa Ludo says.

"You have no idea. We've got to bring the tree back to life. Everything depends on it. Creekside. Me." My fingers caress the space where my arm should be. But now that Grandpa's here, there's a real chance of fixing things—my fingers clamp into a determined fist. "Can you help us?"

Grandpa Ludo looks from me to Mr. Kowalski and finally to the stump. He clears his throat again. "I can try." He reaches into his jacket pocket and pulls out a small, clear bottle no bigger than an acorn. It's filled with clear liquid and capped with a silver lid. "Some people thought Nonna Isabetta was a strega, a witch, as you said, and she may have been, but she was also a woman of faith. She brought this holy water with her across the sea. She used it to bless this land." He shakes the bottle lightly. "In all these years, this holy water has never diminished. A miracle some would call it. I left your father some to fulfill our family's promise, but I see he did not. I consider that my own failure." He unstoppers the lid and hands me the bottle. "Matteo, we can renew that promise and bless this land. As the youngest Lorenzini, will you do this honor?"

I take it from him. The bottle warms in my grip. I actually did it. I brought Grandpa back, and now everything will be okay. I'm so excited I could burst. We'll save the oak.

But then I look down at what Creekside has done to me. My stump is gray brown. A wedge of black cuts into the center rings where the blight had been. They hacked at the trunk so carelessly that the top of the stump is rough and uneven. Instead of caring for me as I have cared for them, they destroyed me. I'm angry and sad because, more than anything, I'm hurt. A tree can't say that it hurts, but a boy can. I look up at Grandpa Ludo and Mr. Kowalski. Their kind faces smile down at me, and I know what I need to do.

I bend and pour three drops on the stump, whispering, "I promise we'll take care of you. That we'll watch over Creekside together . . . and that I'll take better care of myself." The three teardrop shadows fade into the dry, white wood. Nothing happens. I pour some more. I lean closer, whispering so Grandpa Ludo and Mr. Kowalski can't hear me. "I promise there will be no more lies." Still nothing. Getting anxious, I pour until there's nothing left. I hand the empty bottle back to Grandpa Ludo. My heart sinks. "We're too late."

"I was afraid of that," Grandpa Ludo says. His chin dips to his chest mournfully.

"No," Mr. Kowalski says. "Look."

My head snaps up. My eyes widen. From the centermost ring, there's a *p-p-pop* like a nut cracking open. I lean closer. Green breaks through—a stem unfurling like a waking yawn. It's crowned in an emerald bud. My hands are shaking with excitement.

Grandpa Ludo says, "Matteo, you did it!"

Mr. Kowalski rubs his eyes. "It's a miracle!"

I can hardly contain my excitement. I leap up, nearly bowling them over. "Thank you," I say. My arm wraps around Grandpa Ludo. He smells like engine oil and peppermint, so similar to Dad. My stomach knots. "There's more we need to do. Someone else you need to see."

Grandpa Ludo nods. "Will you lead the way?"

I take his hand. Together we leave the park and make our way home to Dad.

SUBJECT: OFFICER IAN JAMES

. . . .

IAN JAMES

Creekside's a special place. It's pure. Innocent. Not too many places like it in the world if you ask me. It needs protecting. That's where I come in.

AZURA GONZALEZ

What does that mean? Why does it need protecting?

IAN JAMES

Pure things are the most vulnerable. I'll do whatever it takes to keep this town safe.

THIRTY-SEVEN

Soon as I step into our front yard, Dad emerges from our house, cell phone pressed to his ear. "He's home. Gotta go." He hangs ups, his eyes only on me. "Matteo, you were supposed to come straight home from school. You had us worried sick."

"Dad, I . . ." But he finally seems to notice that I'm not alone. His whole body goes rigid. His phone slips through his fingers and clatters on the porch. Even with all my tree problems and the town coming after me, I've never seen him react like this. Somewhere between crying and fury. Jaw clenched, he steps down from the stoop.

Grandpa Ludo matches his hesitant step forward. "Hi, Vin."

Dad stops walking. "What are you doing here?"

Mom pokes her head through the front door. "Vinny, is that Matte—oh." Her eyes flash between Grandpa and Dad. She clutches her shirt collar. Slowly she steps outside.

This is legit the most tension I've ever felt. No one moves. I can't imagine what's going on in Dad's mind right now. Is he mad? Upset? What if I messed up? Writing to Grandpa Ludo might have saved the tree and me, but what if I made everything else worse? Will he hate me for asking Grandpa to come home? My breathing speeds up. No. I can't be wrong about this. Dad needs to stop ignoring Grandpa and refusing to tell me the truth about why he left. It's time.

Grandpa Ludo takes another tentative step toward Dad. When Dad doesn't move, he takes another, then another and another. I hold the air tightly in my lungs. Mom's eyes dart between all of us. Dad's hands become fists at his sides. He isn't going to punch Grandpa, is he?

When he's a matter of inches away from Dad, Grandpa Ludo stops. His words come out fragile as glass. "My son, I am so, so sorry." He wraps one arm around Dad, then the other, and pulls him to his chest. The whole time Dad is still, unmoving as stone. The muscles in his face are so taut, veins bulge from his forehead and temples. I'm worried he's going to yell or worse. Then Grandpa Ludo says softly, "I love you, Vin. Please. Forgive me."

A wind passes and Dad collapses into Grandpa's arms like all his bones melted at once. He shakes, crying like I've never seen him before. He looks like a little boy, how I've always imagined I look when *I* cry. My heart swells. I'm so happy they're reunited, but I'm so sad it took this much to get here.

Mom's fingers press against her lips. A tear rolls down her cheek. The tension is gone, and I'm more relieved than I've ever been. I don't cry, but seeing these two grown men hug, both in tears, I know I could full-on sob if I wanted to.

After what feels like forever, they break apart and Grandpa says, "We have a lot to talk about, don't we? May I come in?"

Dad squeezes his shoulder. "Of course. Please. And I— Oh gosh. Dad, meet my wife, Donna." Mom waves at Grandpa. Then Dad points to me. "And it seems like you've already met our son, Matteo."

Grandpa winks at me. "Indeed, I have."

From the sidewalk, Mr. Kowalski says, "I'd better get home. Let you all have your time together."

But Grandpa Ludo stops him. "Too much has separated all of us." He looks to Dad. "Do you mind if Kaz joins?"

I hold my breath. I know Dad knows what this means. He read Grandpa's letters. He'd be inviting Grandpa's old *boyfriend* into our house, who I'm a thousand percent positive he *does* still have feelings for based on their hug-fest in the park.

In this moment, I can't help but think about Omar. Whatever Dad says next isn't just about accepting Grandpa Ludo and Mr. Kowalski. It's also about me.

Dad pauses and, to my surprise, looks at me and smiles.

My cheeks heat up. Does he *know?* He can't. I mean, he *could* but he CAN'T. *I* barely know about me. But then he says to Grandpa Ludo, "Please. Come in. Everyone's welcome." Then he pauses and follows with, "But you and I, old man, we've got some serious talking to do. Man to man."

"Couldn't agree more," Grandpa Ludo says.

Then all of us, Dad, Mom, Grandpa Ludo, Mr. Kowalski, and I, make our way into the house for the longest day of talking, laughing, and crying I have ever known.

CREEKSIDE DOCUMENTARY TRANSCRIPT #37

SUBJECT: STEVIE PRICE

· ·

STEVIE PRICE

The thing about Creekside is that something like having an accident doesn't just go away. Even if it happened a really long time ago. Sometimes knowing everything about everyone is great, but sometimes I wish people knew a little less about me.

AZURA GONZALEZ

Or maybe people can see how far you've come? Since you peed your pants.

STEVIE PRICE

You don't have to keep saying that, but yeah, that would be cool too.

THIRTY-EIGHT

For the first time since my arm snapped off, I actually sleep through the night. The tree's regrowing, even if it's only a little, and Grandpa Ludo and Dad are talking again. But I wake up the next morning with the worst headache. Sharp pain needles the bones behind my eyebrows.

I walk downstairs, hand pressed to my forehead, and find Mom and Dad, still in their pajamas, sitting on the couch with their coffee. Grandpa Ludo and Mr. Kowalski are there too, though they look like they've been up for hours, showered and fully dressed.

Dad sets his cup down. "You okay, sport?"

I grimace. "I slept all right, but my head is throbbing. I don't know what's going on."

Mom pats the seat beside her on the couch. "Let me feel your head."

She presses her cheek to my forehead, then the back of

her hand. "You don't feel warm," she says. "I'll make you some tea."

"Thanks," I say as she shuffles in her slippers to the kitchen. I cozy into the soft cushions next to Dad, pulling a throw blanket over my legs. "I felt better last night, but this morning, I feel like something bad's about to happen."

Dad sets down his mug. "Like what? Is it your other arm? A leg? I thought you said the tree was growing again."

"No, not like that." I press the heels of my palms into my forehead. The pressure eases a little. "It's like . . . like how animals sense a storm coming? That's what it feels like."

"You've had a lot going on," Grandpa Ludo says. "Stress can do weird things to a body."

The stinging behind my eyes burns brighter. "I know, but this feels different."

From the kitchen, Mom says, "Should we call Dr. Wilson?"

"No—" I groan. There's a flash, and in my mind's eye, I see my stump. An overwhelming urge to run to it comes over me. "I need to get to the park."

"Now?" Dad says. "It's barely seven o'clock."

"I know. But something's wrong. We need to get there. Now."

Outside is dreary and gray. Pockets of fog cloud the ground. Grass squishes loudly beneath our feet as we march into the park. From the entrance, I can see exactly what's wrong.

I'm immediately nauseous. The pain in my head doubles.

Mom sees it too. "Vin, look."

"Oh no." Dad grimaces. "You were right, Matteo. Hurry."

The stump has been cordoned off. A team of four workers in white hardhats ready an enormous yellow machine. It looks like something used for road construction, but the tool at the end of the crane has four pincer teeth. There are shovels stuck in the mud too. The roots around the stump have been dug up. The exposed tendrils make it look like an otherworldly octopus rising from the ground.

"Stop! Stop!" Dad hollers, waving his arms. Grandpa Ludo, Mr. Kowalski, Mom, and I chase after him. My heart pounds furiously in my chest. We all shout and beg for them to stop.

Officer James appears from behind the monstrous yellow machine. "Hold your horses there, Vin."

"Ian, please," Dad huffs. "You don't understand. You can't remove the stump."

"Sorry, but it's not up to me. Orders come straight from the mayor's office. I'm just here to oversee security," he says.

I want to scream, my head hurts so bad. My roots, they shouldn't be open to the air like this. This last part of me that's supposed to be safe, buried deep—it's vulnerable to everything.

"We know how it sounds," Mom says, "but Matteo *needs* this stump. *We* need it. If you destroy it—"

Officer James plants his feet firmly in the damp earth. His friendly tone is gone. "There's no argument to be had. Mayor's orders. Besides, this tree should have come out years ago. Look at it. It's more than dead."

"That's not true," I manage. I point to the green stem rising from the bullseye in the stump. "It's coming back to life."

Officer James kneels. His face comes close to mine. I smell the stale cinnamon gum on his breath. "That puny thing? A twig doesn't prove anything."

Mom grips my shoulders, steadying me. "Please," I say. "If you'd just listen."

But Officer James stands with a haughty laugh. "I'm done listening. Everyone's so worked up over this thing!" He turns to Dad and Mom. "It's a *tree*. That's all! A dead tree we've got to remove. Now let's get this show on the road."

Mr. Kowalski pushes through with his wooden cane. "Listen here, Mr. Ian James. You swore to protect this town, and that includes Matteo. You may not understand, but he needs you to do this for him. Now do your job and *protect* him!" He punctuates the last few words by jabbing the stump with his cane.

On the last jab, something strange happens. The cane sticks to the stump. Mr. Kowalski tries to pull it free, but the wood disintegrates to sawdust in his hand and snows all over the stump. We all watch silently, our jaws practically in the grass, Officer James's included. Then the wood dust dissolves into the rings and the young stem shoots up nearly a foot.

Officer James curses loudly.

"You see," I say, seizing the opportunity. "That's proof. It isn't dead. It's special. You can't remove the stump now."

"Ian," Dad says. "Give us a couple days. We'll prove it to you."

Officer James turns back, drawing his hand down his face. "Look, I—I really was just here to check permits and whatnot." He waves a hand over the foot-tall sapling. "I wasn't planning on crowd control, or any of . . . this."

"A day. Give us one day," Mom pleads. "Or even just today. The weather's bad, isn't it? You can do it tomorrow when it's clearer."

Officer James swivels where he stands, like he's weighing the workers and stump on one side with us on the other. His tongue smooths his front teeth. He spits into the dirt.

"Fine. One day," he says. "Tomorrow morning, though, this is gone. Understand?"

My parents nod, but I'm sick to my stomach. That isn't enough time. Even a magic oak can't grow in less than a day!

I slump to the ground. This might be the very last day of my life.

CREEKSIDE DOCUMENTARY TRANSCRIPT #38

SUBJECT: LUDO LORENZINI

• •

LUDO LORENZINI

I've made a lot of mistakes in my life. Most of those stemming from lies I told myself and the ones I love most. Now I've got a chance to make amends for the damage I've done, to myself and my family.

AZURA GONZALEZ

How so?

LUDO LORENZINI

By keeping a promise to be honest. (Coughs) That oak in Creekside Park, it's not just a tree. It's a symbol of who we are. All of Creekside, sure, but us Lorenzinis especially. I used to pride myself on being an upstanding person like the rest of my family, but I let hate and fear and lies take over my life. They came between me and my family, and I failed to keep many promises. Now I've got a chance to make this right, and I don't plan on adding one more tally to my list of mistakes.

THIRTY-NINE

Defeated as I feel, I can't give up now. Not when we were so close to fixing everything. So that afternoon I call a family meeting. And family, I find, means more now than it did a few weeks ago. Gathered around our kitchen table are me, my parents, Grandpa Ludo, Mr. Kowalski, Azura, Omar, and Cricket.

While we eat Dad's famous lemon chicken, which Grandpa Ludo helped him make, I tell everyone what happened earlier that day at the stump with Officer James.

"You're sure it started growing?" Azura asks. She cuts her chicken into tiny squares.

"Positive," I say. "I've been thinking about it all day and I *might* have a way to save my tree." I take a deep breath. "Over the years, branches fell off my oak. People turned my wood into different things: spoons, bats, ladders, shop signs—"

"Rolling pins," Azura chimes in.

"Rolling pins," I repeat. "Even Mr. Kowalski's cane, it turns out. There are parts of me all over town. If we can get enough Creeksiders to bring back whatever the tree—whatever *I* gave them, we might be able to save it. Save me."

Mom gazes at my empty shoulder socket. "Do you think it'll make you whole again?"

"Only one way to find out!" Cricket says cheerfully.

"But Creekside is a mess," says Omar. "And everyone thinks the tree is the problem. Not that you are. You aren't. I'm just saying."

"No, I know," I say. "Which means we need them to understand that I'm *not* the problem. No one knows the truth because I haven't been able to say anything, so everyone thinks the tree's diseased. They think I'm part of the problem. We have to tell everyone about Nonna Isabetta and the magic and the promise."

"Right," Azura muses. "But you can't just get people to believe you."

"People are the worst," says Omar.

"UGH," shouts Cricket. "PEOPLE."

"Okay, so people might be the problem," I say, shushing Cricket, "but they're also the solution. We've got to figure out a way to reach them. Get them to listen."

Mom holds a napkin to her lips while she chews and speaks. "What if we hold a town hall? You, your dad, and I—we can all share our story. Maybe Grandpa Ludo and Mr. Kowalski would be willing to say something too?"

"Anything for you," says Grandpa Ludo. "Of course."

"But how do we get people there?" Dad muses. "And tonight?"

I add, "And would they even listen to us? We can't even get Officer James on our side, and he's one person. Most people think I'm a freak."

"You are *not* a freak," Mom says.

"I know, but that's what people think."

"*Some* people," says Azura.

"Some *losers*," Omar says.

"UGH," says Cricket. "PEOPLE."

I laugh. "I get it, I get it! You all like me." I roll my eyes. "But seriously, what do we do if they won't listen?"

The table quiets. I shove some chicken into my rice. Omar slurps his soda. Cricket swims laps around the overhead lamp. My eyes rove from person to person. Each one of them has a different story. A different connection to me and my tree. Just like everyone else in town . . . That's it! I stand, slamming my fork on the table. "I've got it!"

All eyes turn to me.

"We bribe them with food from Azura's dad's bakery?" Omar asks.

"What? No—although that's not a *terrible* idea." I clear

my throat. "If Creeksiders aren't going to listen to *us*, you know who they might listen to?"

"Who?" asks Azura.

I lay my palm flat on the table, a smug grin spreading over my face. "Themselves."

"That literally doesn't make any sense," says Cricket. "Call the doctor! His brain's rotting from the inside out!"

But Azura seems to put the pieces together. "Our documentary! They *can* listen to themselves. We've got all sorts of video of Creeksiders talking about how much they love the tree."

"Exactly," I say. "If they can just hear themselves and remember all the good that came from the tree, everything it—*I*—have done to watch over them, maybe they'll be willing to help."

"Look," Dad says. "This idea's got legs, but aren't we running into the same problem as before? We might have something to show people, but how do we get it to them? And tonight?"

Omar kicks back in his chair. "*That* you can leave to me and this." He pulls out his cell phone. "Social media was *made* for viral videos, and I've got the hookup. My older brother is legit internet famous. If he posts our video, people will watch. Guaranteed."

"That's perfect." I whip around to Azura. "Can you finish editing the video today?"

She squirms in her chair. "I can try, but it takes a long time."

I smile. "We'll do it together."

"You sure they can't wait longer to remove the stump?" she asks.

"We've been on the phone since this morning trying to convince the mayor's office to postpone the removal," Mom says. "They think we're being overdramatic."

"Well, that settles it." Azura pulls her hair back with a blue tie. "Let's do this. I'm just going to need one final interview." She looks at me.

"Me?" I say.

"I know we said that Creeksiders will listen to themselves, but they also need to hear from you. You deserve to be heard. This is *your* life we're talking about."

"She's right," Dad adds. "Think you're up to recording something?"

Honestly, I'm not feeling up to it at all, but this is my only chance. And I agree with them. I have the right to be heard. Now that I'm a boy, and not just a tree, I have a voice too. I can't let that go to waste. "I'll do it."

Azura doesn't wrap up editing the video until almost seven o'clock. I know I'm biased, but the way she stitched together interviews from Dorothy Van Otten all the way to Stevie Price is amazing. Hearing everyone come together, including Mayor Meyers, talking about how the oak is the town's heart and soul, makes me feel like we have a real chance at saving the stump. Watching my clip at the very end, with my family and friends all around me, talking about what the tree and Creekside mean to me (explaining *very* clearly that I *am* the tree), it makes me a little anxious but prouder than anything. I'm putting myself out there just as I am. *Because* of who I am. The video proves that everyone in town knew the oak was special; they just didn't know *how* special until now. I just hope the video's enough to change what happens tomorrow.

When Omar's brother posts the video to his social media accounts, he lets Omar know that his phone immediately started buzzing with notifications.

"That's a good sign," Grandpa Ludo says. "Right?"

"As long as people listen," says Omar. "Yeah, it's a really good thing."

I hug him and Azura extra long when they leave. I want to remember what it feels like to hold them close in case this is the last chance I get.

"It's all going to work out," Azura whispers in my ear. "You'll see."

"I hope so."

Omar grabs my hand. My skin tingles. He's never done this before. Well, not held my *hand* hand. He squeezes and says, "We're with you. No matter what."

I squeeze back. "Thanks."

When my friends, Grandpa Ludo, and Mr. Kowalski are gone, I can't sleep. Neither can Mom and Dad. Our minds are trapped in a whirlpool of worry. Even Cricket floats over us like a rain cloud. We sit on the couch, holding each other close, and wait for dawn, knowing that, at the very least, right now, in this moment, we have each other and that is a beautiful thing.

FORTY

It's still dark when Dad gently shakes me awake. I must have fallen asleep nestled between him and Mom. I yawn, taking in the faces of the people who love me most in the world. Mom's hair is unevenly flattened where her head came to rest on the couch. Shadows kiss her cheeks, and red veins fill in the whites of her eyes, but she's smiling. Dad looks equally as exhausted. He hasn't shaved in days and a peppery beard coats his face. He pushes himself up from the couch, stretching his arms to the ceiling.

"I want to get there before anyone else," he says. "No one is taking you away from us."

My legs are weak, but I rise beside him. "Let's do this."

We quickly brush our teeth and eat, keeping on the clothes we wore the day before. Then we throw on jackets and shoes and make our way out the door. I haven't seen Cricket at all this morning, and that makes me especially nervous. If he's gone, does that mean the tree is getting worse? Does that mean I'll disappear too? I look back at our house, wondering if this is the last time I'll ever see it.

The overcast weather hasn't let up. The sky is heavy with gray clouds. Earthworms clog the sidewalks. I avoid trampling them as we near the Creekside Park archway. We walk through, and Mom takes my hand. Her fingers are chilled, but heat blooms between our palms. I hold her tight. I never want to let go.

We near the hill and my heart gallops beneath my ribs. Fear pumps furiously through every inch of me. I hold Mom's hand tighter when I see what lies ahead.

Men and women in hard hats beat us to the stump. It looks like they've been here awhile, even though the mayor's office assured Mom they wouldn't get started until close to eight o'clock. Officer James is among them, circling the exposed roots. His face is one hard line. When he sees us coming, he shakes his head in annoyance. "You folks just don't give up, do you?"

"Ian, we're talking about my *son*," says Dad.

Officer James chuckles. "Right, right. I saw the video. Couple of the guys sent it to me last night. You really think Matteo's a tree? Come on, Vin. You've got to be kidding me."

I find my voice. "I know it's hard to understand, but it's the truth. I *am* the tree. The whole town is connected to me, whether you want to believe it or not."

He rolls his eyes. "Give me a break." He looks from me

to my parents. "You all can't really be buying this."

"You saw it grow yesterday," Mom says. "Why isn't that enough for you?"

I bite my lip. There's got to be a way to convince him that we're telling the truth. I kick off my shoes, ignoring Mom and Dad when they ask what I'm doing. I dig my toes into the grass until they reach the muddy earth and take root.

"What are you doing?" Officer James says, but I ignore him too.

I reach and reach until I find what I'm looking for. My roots.

Help me, I beg. *Give me something I can use to save us.*

Underground, the old roots shift. They bend to me. My insides warm. There's still hope. "I can show you the truth." I extend my hand to Officer James. My fingers grow. A leaf unfurls from each fingertip.

His eyes widen. "That's impossible." A shadow comes over him. "I'm not buying it. It's a nice trick, but I have my orders." He shouts to the workers. "Dig this up. Now."

I sink to my knees, woozy. Those leaves took more out of me than I realized they would. And even that wasn't enough.

"No!" Mom cries.

Dad lunges at the stump, covering it with his whole body. "You can't do this," he says.

"Don't make me arrest you," says Officer James. "I'll do it. Don't test me."

"He's just a kid," Dad says.

"And this is just a tree. That's all. Stop acting like it's more than that!"

The yellow machine's engine revs. The noise reminds me of the chainsaws that came before it. The pincers open like a monstrous jaw. Mom holds me to her.

"I'm not moving," Dad shouts back.

Officer James doesn't say another word. He grabs Dad around the waist and, in one swift jerk, pulls him from the stump. Dad fights back for a moment but then seems to remember he's wrestling a police officer and gives in. Officer James pins his hands behind his back.

The pincers lower. Mom hugs me so tight I can hardly breathe, but I don't want her to stop. Not for one second.

I flinch when the metal teeth bite the stump. Each one tears into the wood, and I can feel the sharp, cold grip on my skin. My eyes sting. Everything hurts.

Officer James shouts, "Do it."

FORTY-ONE

"No! Wait!"

Azura runs up the hill, Omar at her heels. In her hand is the wooden rolling pin from her dad's bakery. Then Mr. Gonzalez appears behind her in his apron. Ms. Geraldo is with him. They're shouting for the machines to stop, but it's too late. One rolling pin isn't going to change anything, especially if there's no stump left to give anything back to.

"What now?" Officer James grumbles. He lets up on Dad's wrists, twisting to get a better view of the new arrivals.

Azura kneels beside me and Mom. "It's going to be all right, Matteo," she says. "They're coming. For *you*."

I'm in so much pain, I'm struggling to process what she's saying. "What? Who?"

"You'll see," Omar says, right beside her. "We've got to do something else first."

"Come on," Azura says.

My friends dash to the stump. Officer James leaps after

them, releasing Dad. "Get away from there," he shouts. "It's dangerous!"

But they charge ahead and wedge the rolling pin between the metal teeth. The reaction is instant. The rolling pin turns to dust, and the yellow machine groans. For a heartbeat, I think the machine is yanking the stump from the dirt again, but I quickly realize it's the opposite. The stump is fighting its way back into the earth, taking the machine down with it.

"Uhh, Officer James?" the man behind the machine calls. "Something funky's going on."

Branches of rich brown bark burst through the machine's blades. The growth snakes around the metal teeth. The surface of the stump begins to disappear, covered in fresh wood. My roots shake, both those open to the sky and those below the earth. I draw in air. My lungs expand with ease. "It's working," I say to Mom. "But we need more."

"Pull that thing out now!" Officer James shouts.

But the worker behind the machine is gone. He leaped away when the vining branches crushed one of the metal teeth.

"This is ridiculous!" Officer James spits. "I'll do it myself."

He jumps behind the controls and kicks the engine to life. The machine screeches. He pulls a lever, and the now three-toothed jaw ascends, dragging the remains of the oak with it. The branches woven around the teeth snap. I slump to the ground, wrapping my arms around my legs. I feel so small and helpless. Everything hurts.

"Matteo!" Mom cries, but her voice sounds far off.

The gears in the machine grind furiously. And then Omar shouts, "They're here!"

My vision is blurry, but there are shapes of people climbing the hill. Their hands are full. Grandpa Ludo and Mr. Kowalski are the first to reach us. Then Coach Mathis, Ms. Grainger, and Mrs. Mandrake. Mrs. Curtis from Conehead's. Dorothy Van Otten with her cats weaving between her legs. Omar's parents and his brother. Guys from the team: Jimmy Briar and Miguel Ruiz and Freddie McCoy. Even Tyler Sudbury. Creeksiders from every corner of town have come, some I've never spoken to as a boy but all I've known as a tree.

Each person has brought something with them to place at the roots of my tree. The old ladder from the fire station. The sign from the coffee shop. Pressed leaves and bunches of ancient acorns. Little whittled birds and gnome figurines. A picture frame made of twigs. Wooden dolls and wooden spoons and wooden bowls. They all turn to dust, and the stump absorbs all of it. My strength is returning. I push myself to standing, watching as the half-tree snaps through the jaws of the machine. Officer James curses loudly, smashing his fists on the control panel.

He's so furious, so unwilling to see what's happening

before his eyes, that he doesn't notice the branch swing at his head. It crashes into him, and his unconscious body flumps over on the metal monster. I don't *think* I did that on purpose, but I'm perfectly okay that he's out cold.

Now all my attention is on my tree. The stump nestles back into the earth. Mud and dirt cake over my roots. For the first time that day, I get a taste of safety.

Then there's a loud groan, and a glorious trunk, as thick and wide as it had once been, soars into the gray sky. The assembled Creeksiders gasp in awe. Cocoa-brown bark glistens in the morning light. We all watch, mouths agape. Grandpa Ludo, Mr. Kowalski, Azura, and Omar gather close. I hold my parents to me, watching this thing that I was, and somehow still am, be reborn.

But the trunk stops growing before leafy branches can appear. Anxious whispers flit through the crowd. My heart skips a beat.

"What's happening?" Mom asks. "Why did it stop?"

"I need more," I say, knowing it's the truth.

Dad looks dismayed. "All we have left is the family bat. Is that going to be enough?"

As if in response, something glowing yellowish-greenish zooms through the air and lands at my feet: my broken off arm. Dr. Wilson had taken it with her. I thought I'd never see it again. It stops glowing and Cricket floats out of it.

"You're okay," I gasp with relief.

"You bet your gills I am," he says. "I just figured you could use a hand this morning." He chuckles. "The rest of the arm's a bonus."

Of course. My arm—I *am* the tree. There is something else we can give. I beam at Cricket. I couldn't love him more. "This is perfect. Thank you."

With my right hand, I scoop up my severed arm. I look at Dad, "Can you grab the bat?"

"Sure thing," he says, following behind.

The closer we get to the tree, the stronger I feel the oak's warmth. The heat of energy. Of life. I raise my broken arm to the trunk. Dad does the same with the bat. In a gust, they dissolve into the bark. The tree expands once more. Higher up, the trunk splits, a cascade of naked branches forking in every direction. But the tree stops again, and I falter. I was so sure that would be enough.

"Maybe it needs time," Dad says.

But in my heart, I know exactly what it needs. "No. That's not it." I step forward and place my hand on the bark. My skin flares with heat. It tickles my palm. There's only one option left. I smile sadly back at him. "It needs me."

Dad grabs my shoulder, his face drawn. "No, Matteo. You are not sacrificing yourself."

I glance back at Mom, who's standing next to Grandpa Ludo. They're both crying. I hate that they're sad, but this is the only way. I look back at Dad and say, "After all this time,

I finally know who I am. I know what I am. And I'm happy with it. I love all of it. All of me." The words are true, but I can't help tearing up because, really, I don't know what happens after this. All I know is that this is what has to happen. "This isn't a sacrifice," I say. "It's a gift."

"You can't go," he says, a tear dripping down his cheek.

I smile. "I'm not going anywhere." My eyes wander into the leafless branches. "I'll be where I've always been."

Mom approaches, fingers at her lips. "I didn't want to believe you were anything other than our son." Her eyes lift from me to the oak. "But you're so much more than the son I ever dreamed I'd have. I see that now. You *are* magic, Matteo." She takes my hand, and I almost lose my nerve. Then she says to Dad, "Vin, we haven't listened to him for weeks, but we can now."

Dad's face twists uncertainly. "Donna, we can't—"

"Yes." Mom lets go of me and takes Dad's hand. "We can."

He stares into her eyes for a long time. Then his chest shudders, like he's holding in a sob. I can't stand seeing them in pain. I almost call it all off, just to make the hurting stop, but Dad nods several times at Mom and then pulls me into a vise-grip hug. "We love you. So much, Matteo."

"I know," I say. Mom's arms fold around both of us. "I love you too."

When we let go of each other, I look back at Grandpa Ludo and Mr. Kowalski, Coach Mathis and my teachers,

Dorothy, the Blue Whales, Mr. Gonzalez and Ms. Geraldo, the Joneses, and at last, Cricket, Omar, and Azura. My friends. My very best friends.

Without another word, I let go of Dad and press myself to the tree. My skin warms and heat floods my bones. I become weightless. A feather. A leaf. Suddenly, there's nothing to me at all. I am dust. There is a tremendous groan, and the oak explodes with leaves. I find that I'm no longer standing on the ground. I am below it and towering above it. I am bark and stem. I am every strong, steady bough. I am each radiant, glistening green leaf. A wind, warm and soft as a baby's breath, hushes through my leaves and over the crowd.

At long last, I am whole.

FORTY-TWO

I am an oak tree. I am a boy.

Both, magically and magnificently, all at the same time. There is such strength in these wooden limbs. Power. Fortitude. Once more a tree, I can give of myself to Creekside. I can take care of everyone. I can keep the promise I made to Isabetta Lorenzini all those years ago.

Then I see my parents' faces. Grandpa Ludo and Mr. Kowalski. Azura and Omar. Cricket. Their eyes roam my branches and my trunk as if they expect my face to appear in the rivulets of bark. I want to tell them I'm okay, that I already miss them. I desperately want to hug Mom and Dad. To assure them I'm not gone. Not really. I want to celebrate with Azura and Omar. We *did* it. We restored the tree. I want to confide in Cricket, to tell him all about what it's like, being a tree who is a boy who is a tree.

But that's the thing about trees. They don't have voices to shout "I love you" or arms to hug. Instead, I have branches to shade and a trunk to lean against. I have acorns and leaves to feed. But those things seem to matter less now that I know what it's like to walk on two legs.

As the minutes extend into hours, Creeksiders leave in pairs and trios. From high up, I watch them pass under the Creekside Park archway. They return to their breakfasts and their jobs and their schools. Their feet pad sidewalks and streets and carpets. My roots stretch beneath them all, listening, taking it all in. They whisper my name. They say it sadly. They say it with awe. They say it with regret. But I cannot say anything back.

Midmorning, Grandpa Ludo and Mr. Kowalski shuffle off, their eyes red. Omar and Azura follow after them, consoled by their parents. I don't want any of them to leave. I want them to climb and laugh and play.

Watching them live their lives outside the park—it isn't enough, but it will have to be. I'm where I'm supposed to be. I'll provide for them. They'll see. I'll watch over them and protect them.

By noon, only my parents remain, huddled under my shady branches. Dad wraps himself around Mom. Then Mom wraps herself around Dad. They take turns mourning. Grandpa Ludo and Mr. Kowalski return with food and water for them, but they act like they hardly notice. All they seem concerned with is how my leaves shift overhead.

How I creak in the wind. How my shadow lengthens on the grass as the sun sets.

The moon appears in the sherbet sky, and still they don't go. Yellow and orange and red melt into starry violet night. Stars wink. A cool breeze replaces the warmth of the day.

Finally, at long last, they drag themselves away from me. I never could have imagined it would hurt this much watching them leave.

FORTY-THREE

Thursday. A new day. I'm growing strong, but part of me worries that the mayor or Officer James will return to chop me down. But no one does. Mom and Dad come back. They bring thermoses of coffee. Grandpa Ludo and Mr. Kowalski sit with them in lawn chairs. They talk and laugh and cry. They tell me the town is looking and feeling normal again, but that it means nothing without me beside them.

Friday. It rains. Azura and Omar visit me after school, huddled under a large purple umbrella. Azura tells me our video has gotten all sorts of likes and reposts on social media. How even Mayor Meyers is talking up the screening of our full documentary at the bicentennial celebration. Omar says tomorrow's baseball game won't be the same without me. That they'll probably lose because I'm not there. I wish I could laugh. Then they ask me to come back. To find a way to be a boy again. I want to tell them that I wish I could, but I made a choice. I'm keeping a promise. I wish they could see that.

Saturday. Instead of sitting in the stands and cheering on the Blue Whales, Mom and Dad keep me company. They tell me about how they've been. Mom says she can't sleep without knowing I'm in the house. Dad says he misses the sound of my feet coming down the stairs. Mom says the dinner table is too quiet without me chomping in her ear. Dad says he doesn't know what to do after work without me there to play catch with him. My heartwood breaks with each word they speak, but I can't help them the way they want.

Sunday. Monday. Tuesday. Before I was a boy, I never realized how long a day really was. When you're a tree, a day passes the way a minute does for a person. But now that I've known a human day, a human minute, a human second, I cannot go back to knowing time like I did before. Now I know that the people I love, the people I most want to talk to and laugh with and wrap my arms around and walk alongside, do not have days the way I do. Their minutes are fleeting. I miss them, and I am missing time to be with them. These precious days and minutes and seconds. Being a tree has brought life back to Creekside, but it's taken so much from me.

Wednesday. A week has gone by. This day, I decide, is

a tall tree watching over the other days of the week. It's the week's center, its heart. This day, it is *my* day. I am still growing strong, but my boughs are heavy. Mom and Dad come to visit each and every day, but I'm getting tired of not being able to talk to them. Of only ever being able to watch. I miss them.

That afternoon, Grandpa Ludo climbs the little hill alone to talk with me.

"Matteo," he says. "I hope you can hear me." He rests his back against my trunk and slides down. He sits with his hands in the grass. "What you did, to restore the town, even when most of them couldn't see the gift you were giving them—it's admirable. Creekside's as good as it ever was. I wish you could see it."

My leaves flutter. *I can. I see it every minute of every day.*

"Your parents, though," he goes on. "They aren't the same without you. It's like—it's like someone pulled out all their organs and replaced their insides with wires and gears. They're robots when they're not here talking to you." He sniffs. "Now, I've got something to say, and I need you to hear me. I've lived a long life, and I've learned a few things. First and foremost, you cannot live for other people. You do that, and you'll miss living your own life."

He takes a deep breath. I wait. I listen.

He goes on, "Second, I know what it means to run away because you think you're doing the right thing, because you think that being gone from the ones you love is what's best for everyone." He coughs into his hand. I don't let a single leaf move. These are important words. He goes on: "Matteo, please don't make the same mistakes I did. Don't miss out on what is right in front of you." He pushes himself up, pressing his hands against my bark. "I guess what I'm saying is, two things can be true at the exact same time. You can be exactly who you are and be loved. You can be a boy *and* a tree. And this time, your family will be there to support you, exactly as you are."

He pats my trunk and shuffles off. I watch him the whole way out of the park.

Two things can be true at the exact same time.

I am an oak tree. I am a boy.

Grandpa Ludo is right. That *is* what I want. To be both. To be the most that I can be. To be exactly what I am and not have to pretend or hide. To be loved for all of me.

Suddenly, I am filled with a wild, raging heat. It starts in my heartwood and permeates through every ring. It soars into my branches and sizzles into every cell of every leaf. It burrows underground through every forking root. And I realize this is my chance. I am full of the warmth of life, the blessing Isabetta Lorenzini bestowed upon me two hundred years ago. This is my chance to change my fate. I burn hotter and hotter, blindingly so. So alarmingly warm that I'm afraid I might actually ignite.

When I gave myself back to the tree, I thought I didn't have a choice. But I was wrong. I didn't understand or realize what was possible because I was so worried and rushed and scared. But Grandpa Ludo is showing me a different way. He's right. I *can* be everything I want to be all at the same time. I am so excited, I might burst.

I pour all my energy into a single wish. Every leaf, every branch, every bit of bark vibrates with the thrill of possibility.

Finally, I'm ready to become who I was always meant to be.

I am filled with a blazing crescendo of magic. Then, as quickly as it began, the crackling heat fades, and I find that I can't see from as high up as before. In fact, I'm kind of short for a tree. And my branches aren't so long or quite as many. No. That's not right. I don't have branches at all. Or roots. I have feet. I have legs. And a body and hair and two whole arms. My heart—*my heart*—it drums in my chest. My face stretches wide with a smile. I can hardly believe it.

This is who I was always meant to be. I am an oak tree and a boy. Both at once. Both true. Finally, I'm standing on my own two feet, sure that I'm growing into the person I want to be. And I don't waste another day, another minute, another second waiting to find the people I love most in this whole wide world.

EPILOGUE

Azura screams from the stands. "You can do it, Matteo!"

I give her a thumbs-up. It's the bottom of the ninth in the final game before the summer season starts. We're having a rematch with the Amber Owls, who have six runs to our four. Tyler and Miguel stand on second and third respectively. With two outs already on the board, this game is going to be our closest yet.

I step up to home plate clutching an aluminum bat between my sweaty palms.

Omar cheers me on from behind the chain-link fence, along with a few of the other Blue Whales. Even Tyler gives me a whistle. Funny how things change when people see you for who you really are.

The Amber Owl on the pitcher's mound hikes up and throws the ball. I swing.

"Strike one," the umpire calls.

"That's all right, Matteo," Dad shouts. "Deep breaths."

317

"You've got this," Mom says.

I wink over my shoulder at them. They're both wearing giant, goofy grins, and when they see me looking, they both shoo my attention back to the pitcher who is already winding up for the second pitch.

"Hit that ball, Matteo! Right over the fence!" Grandpa Ludo shouts.

He's with Mr. Kowalski, who now insists on us calling him Kaz. They're sitting in matching lawn chairs, holding hands. They each have a water bottle with their name written on it in permanent marker. Their knees touch. Thanks to them, I had the courage to tell Mom and Dad the truth about my feelings for Omar. I didn't think it was possible for them to love me more, but it seems like they do. Or maybe it's just that I'm finally letting them know all of me.

The pitcher's arm pulls back. I hunker down. The ball flies at me. I swing!

"Strike two!"

"Come on, Matteo," Azura cheers. "Knock it out of the park!"

"Don't be such a baby about it," Tyler hollers. "Smack that sucker!"

The pitcher winds back his arm for the final pitch. I exhale through my nose, planting my feet firmly on the ground. I can't help a mischievous grin.

"You ready for this?" I whisper.

Cricket appears from underneath my helmet. "When am I ever *not* ready?"

He hasn't let up haunting me one bit. We both prefer it that way.

"Let's do this," I say.

The pitcher hurls the ball. As soon as my bat connects with it, Cricket zips into the baseball and takes off, arching wide into the air.

Wild, uproarious cheers peal from the stands. I bolt from home plate, remembering to drop the bat this time. I sprint past first, wind rippling over my skin. Dad shouts, "That's our son! That's our son!"

And that's my dad, I think. *That's my dad. My mom. My grandpas. My friends.*

That's my family.

The Cricket-possessed baseball lands somewhere out in left field. Each time an Amber Owl tries to pluck it out of the grass, it rolls away, *almost* as if it has a mind of its own. I'm dying laughing as I run. The Amber Owls look ridiculous, chasing the ball like cats after a superpowered mouse.

Before I realize it, I'm dashing past second base, my heart thundering in my chest. Out of the corner of my eye, I see Tyler's already run in and Miguel isn't far behind.

The cheers grow louder. I rocket past third. Miguel is panting just past home plate. Tyler hollers for me to run harder. Omar whoops from the dugout. My stomach flutters. Maybe I'll tell him how I really feel today. Maybe. But right now, I've got to push with everything I've got.

Off to my left, the ball rolls all over the place, zigzagging in corkscrews and lightning bolts and figure eights. *Cricket is loving this,* I think.

Then the ball comes to a sudden stop. Three Amber Owls dog pile on top of it.

But it's too late.

I've made it.

I'm home.

ACKNOWLEDGMENTS

This book began as a seed of a thought while I was working on my master's degree at Vermont College of Fine Arts back in 2019. Amy King, my wonderful advisor at the time, helped me nurture and prune Matteo's story into what became my creative thesis. That version of Matteo is very different from the pages you hold today, but I will be forever grateful to Amy for giving my little tree boy the water and sunlight he needed to first branch out and find his voice.

This book also holds a very special place in my heart because it brought me to Sara Crowe, the most wonderful, amazing agent a writer could ask for. She championed this story from the beginning—I remember our first phone call where we both dreamed about seeing Cricket on a cover someday. I'm beyond happy that day is here and now. Thank you, thank you for all you do.

Thank you, too, to all the folks at Pippin for their time and energy: Holly McGhee, Elena Giovinazzo, Ashley Valentine, Marissa Brown, and Morgan Hughes.

My heart is so full of gratitude for my extraordinary

editor, Stephanie Stein, who found the heartwood of this novel and helped me see how the roots could go deeper, the branches stretch higher, and the leaves shine brighter. You are absolute gem.

I am so grateful to all the individuals at HarperCollins who put their time, energy, skills, and talents into this book, especially Sophie Schmidt, Jon Howard, Gwen Morton, Sean Cavanagh, Vanessa Nuttry, Corina Lupp, Delaney Heisterkamp, Sammy Brown, Patty Rosati, Mimi Rankin, and Christina Carpino.

A book is not complete without fabulous cover art, and the immensely talented Ariel Vittori brought Matteo and his friends to life so beautifully. Thank you, Ariel, for yet another stunning, eye-catching illustration.

I have so many incredible writers in my life who inspire and guide me. Thank you to the Guardians of Literary Mischief, especially Sarah Willis and Adina Baseler, who are my dear friends and critique partners.

I am so grateful to the Turth Machine (not a typo) for their constant love and support. An extra shout-out to Alina Borger-Germann and Mary Winn Heider who read early drafts and shared fantastic feedback with me.

Thank you to the Beverly Shores crew who see me, love me, and cheer me on.

I will be forever grateful to the educators who helped me grow into the writer and person I am today. I want to shout out Tracey Contino, one of my fantastic high school English teachers, who taught me the power of metaphor. Thank you for continuing to teach me and be such a wonderful friend.

Thank you, as well, to the faculty and staff at Vermont College of Fine Arts. My time at VCFA continues to have a profound impact on my life. I will be forever grateful to my advisors Will Alexander, David Gill, Kekla Magoon, and Amy King.

I am so grateful to my students, past and present, who continue to inspire me to tell stories that help them to feel seen and to better see others.

Thank you to all the librarians, educators, and booksellers who share my stories and all stories about marginalized identities with readers of all ages. You are so needed and so appreciated. More than words can truly express.

Thank you to my dear friends who check in on me and make me laugh as I write my stories. I couldn't do this work without you.

Most importantly, I want to thank my family for always being my biggest cheerleaders and support. My mom gets an extra shout-out for always being one of my very first readers. I love you all very much.

Finally, thank you, dear reader. I'm so grateful that you are here, right now, reading these words. You are a gift. Never forget that.